EMPIRE OF
RISE

RISE OF REBELS

By
Tarik Bouchnayf

Copyright © 2023

All rights reserved; no part of this publication may be reproduced or transmitted by any means, electronic, mechanical, photocopying, or otherwise, without the prior permission of the publisher.

Table of Contents

Chapter 1 5

Chapter 2 14

Chapter 3 22

Chapter 4 32

Chapter 5 43

Chapter 6 48

Chapter 7 54

Chapter 8 65

Chapter 9 73

Chapter 10 84

Chapter 11 92

Chapter 12 101

Chapter 13 115

Chapter 14 127

Chapter 15 137

Chapter 16 146

Chapter 17 159

Chapter 18 174

Chapter 19 184

Chapter 20 192

Chapter 21 201

Chapter 22 211

Chapter 23 223

Chapter 24 234

Chapter 25 241

Chapter 26 249

Chapter 27 261

Chapter 28 280

CHAPTER 1

With the capture of the last true king, all hope seemed lost. Deposed and alone, King Eleah could only flee and beg aid from old allies. But many had turned their backs, aiding in his capture by the Empire's ruthless commander. The party rode on, weary from the journey but driven by the promise of a hefty reward from the emperor for the capture of their prized prisoner.

The dense forest and ominous clouds loomed above, mirroring the dark fate that awaited the fallen king at the Empire's stronghold.

Ali couldn't let that happen. He had followed the Empire's soldiers since they entered the forbidden forest, waiting for the right moment to attack; the heavy rain helped him approach without drawing attention. Still, every step taken was predetermined. If his foot caught on a branch, he would have to deal with over twenty soldiers. Time didn't help him either, as in less than two miles, the soldiers will reach the bridge, and it will be too late to save the fallen king.

King Eleah wasn't the first to be sentenced to death: many innocent people had paid the price with their lives for not bending their knees to the emperor, and Ali had watched them being escorted to the execution yard. Every day, Ali remembered the blood pooling on the chopping block, and the thud as their heads rolled to the ground. He couldn't save them; he couldn't bring them back. But he did remember them, and pity infiltrated his heart every time he did.

Although Ali was a courageous man and a fierce fighter, he was aware of how powerless he was against the forces of the Empire. So he had worked in the shadows until Eleah was arrested, sooner ready to die rather than let the last legitimate king be executed for refusing to bend the knee to the emperor.

The detained king was ready to die, but Ali couldn't let that happen. The condemned king was the only legitimate heir left to rule on earth. Killing him would make the little hope left in Ali's heart go out.

Ali seldom felt lucky, but that day in particular, luck decided to smile upon him.

The soldiers' leader stopped and spoke to one of his men, "Go and inform the emperor that we're coming with the traitor. Half of you, come with me."

The soldiers took their way, and Ali couldn't believe that he had been left with ten fighters instead of twenty-one; still, it was hard to fight all these men by himself, but life taught him the higher risk a man takes, the more reward he gets.

Deep down, Ali hesitated to attack. The Thinkers had advised him not to, and Ali never disobeyed them except in this matter, when he chose to follow his heart.

He finally revealed himself, standing in the soldiers' way with a black hood covering his head.

"This way is closed, only dead people can pass," Ali warned.

The room erupted in laughter as the commander declared, "Today is full of surprises, a traitor and a rebel in one day!" And with a barked command to "Seize him!" the soldiers advanced on Ali, who swiftly unsheathed two daggers and hurled them at his attackers. Two men fell, but three more rushed forward. Ali, a blur of motion, whipped out his sword and cut down one man without hesitation. Spinning around, he caught the second soldier coming up behind him and sliced through his belly. The third soldier, horrified by the sight of his comrade's entrails, froze, and Ali dispatched him with two swift blows.

With a fierce determination in his eyes, Ali refused to let his comrades flee in the face of danger. With lightning-quick precision, he launched two more daggers at the remaining enemies, felling them in an instant. He then turned his attention to their leader, a towering figure looming twenty feet away, bow and arrow at the ready.

"Surrender now, and reveal your face," the commander commanded, his voice filled with menace.

With a sly grin, Ali removed his hood, revealing his true identity. The commander's expression twisted into one of horror and betrayal as he exclaimed, "You! Traitor!"

But before the commander could shoot his arrow, a sharp sound echoed through the battlefield as a chain wrapped around his neck from behind, nearly choking the life from him. As the commander gasped for air, Eleah, who had been captured and held prisoner, emerged from behind him, sword in hand. With a swift, merciless strike, he plunged the blade into the commander's heart, ending his reign of terror forever.

The deposed king looked at Ali and gasped, "I couldn't let you do all the killings yourself."

"The last thing I enjoy is killing people," Ali said while unchaining him. The legitimate king was released, and he quickly put a sword on Ali's neck. "Give me a good reason not to kill you."

"Not if I kill you first," boasted Ali.

The king felt a pointed object about to pierce his kidney; he slowly took his sword off and asked, "Seriously, how many daggers do you carry?"

As he turned, Ali handed him a dagger, and to the king's surprise it was his own. He kept it hidden inside his robe.

Ali smirked. "I usually carry four, and yours is the fifth,"

The king glowered. "You might be a smart knight, but not good enough to make a fool of me."

"Is that how you thank someone who saved your life?"

"You think I care about my life?" replied the king.

"You care enough to carry a dagger in your cloak!" Ali said.

"I have no time to play games with you," the king eyed Ali up and down. "What does a man like you want with me?

"Your grace, you're the only man who can restore peace on earth."

The king looked at him, surprised, and Ali knew he got his attention, "You have every reason not to trust me. You've been betrayed by the closest men to you." The king kept staring at Ali as he spoke, "I always consider that trust is something to be earned, not be asked for, but I need to ask you to trust me!"

"And why should I grant you this exception?"

Ali put his sword back on its sheath and took two steps toward the king, "Because I don't trust you either. Many deposed kings revolted in the beginning and ended up bending their knees to the emperor! But I choose to take a risk because I don't have a choice. You're my only chance to have a different world. Perhaps you should trust that I'm the only help you've got."

Eleah didn't say a word and Ali continued, "Unless you have an army waiting for you to place you on your throne?"

Somehow the words reached the king's heart, but he doubted that the man in front of him was aware of the power of his enemy. His tone was dry as he spoke, "And

I'm supposed to believe that you're the one who will get me my crown back?"

"Maybe. I reached my first goal, which was to save the last legitimate king on earth," enthused Ali, "That counts for something!"

"And who do you want me to rule while everyone answers to the Empire?" asked the king.

"Those who are consumed by fear," replied Ali. "When you secure a land and start raising an army, the fear in some hearts will turn into courage, and they will join from every corner of the world."

King Eleah realized that Ali wasn't as naïve as he thought, so he decided to give him a chance and trust him. After all, the deposed king had nothing to lose, and it was a good call because, after three days of riding, they reached the sea.

To the king's surprise, Ali had already prepared a boat and explained that the only safe option they had was to disappear from the Empire's sight.

One place that the Empire's soldiers could never reach was an island called the Haunted Land. No one ever dared to sail to it, and many stories were whispered about the resident evil there. When Ali told the king about it, he expected it to awaken his superstitious side, but there was none left; he was even glad to go there.

"I always wanted to visit this place!" exclaimed the king.

Ali released the boat and got in with his new companion.

The sea was a mystery to Eleah. For starters, its color constantly changed from blue to gray during the day and then turned to black and white at night. Its taste was also puzzling, the salt which was one of the flavors that people love most, yet a thirsty man couldn't drink even one sip from it. But the thing that twisted his mind most was the life there; giant and tiny creatures that could live in the water for a lifetime, while a human couldn't survive a few minutes underwater. After a while, he couldn't see the land they left, nor their destination, just a breathtaking view of the blue sky reflected in the water, and a complete silence broken by the sound of the boat paddling.

Their journey lasted two days, and they only talked about one thing: the Empire. When they arrived, Eleah stood and started contemplating the view of the island. He heard many scarring stories about it, but the greenery he saw suggested that its land was full of life.

Then again, he knew how appearances could fool even the wisest people. "Is it true that this island is haunted?" he asked.

"I can't tell. I have never seen anything that suggested such a thing. But I also know that I didn't see everything on this island last time I came," replied Ali with a smile.

After that, Ali took two small rocks to start a fire. Eleah thought he wanted to dry his clothes, but he didn't. Instead, fetched an arrow from his quiver, lit the head, and shot it far away. Eleah asked immediately why he had done that.

"You'll find out very soon," replied Ali.

After walking three miles, the king spotted smoke and wondered if it was the arrow that Ali had thrown. Moments later, he heard voices, then saw a few people dressed in black. They sounded like guards from the way they were standing; it didn't stop there. Eleah began seeing tents and children running and playing. He could see clearly that the island was inhabited.

Ali said no word until they got in a tent, where dozens of men and women were gathered.

Ali put his arms out, waving to the people. "Your grace, what do you think about your new kingdom?"

Eleah was in shock: for starters, the island that he had spent his entire life wondering about its mysteries turned out to be a village with a unique population; he saw people from all ethnicities, and he couldn't hide his emotions.

"Your grace," Ali said, "these people have suffered from the Empire's injustice, and they decided to act; they didn't carry swords or set traps, they chose to leave the tyranny of the emperor and look for a better life. That courage is no different from yours or mine."

After a long silence, Eleah asked a series of questions: "How did you bring them here? And how many are they? And …"

"I told you; I've been working in the shadows for over five years," smiled Ali.

Eleah finally placed the emotion he had. A smile broke out on his face, the men and women inside the tent were relieved to see him happy. He asked them one by one for their names, kingdoms, and how they ended up there, and they all answered enthusiastically.

The king turned to Ali and asked him if they could speak in private, and they both exited the tent and went next to a tree.

"You're engraving a glorious history, Ali," acknowledged Eleah while they were walking. "Together, you and I can build a new world!"

Ali sighed. "Your grace, I'm afraid I can't stay here."

Eleah didn't open his mouth. Instead, he kept looking at Ali, waiting for him to elaborate. "We have three thousand and forty-eight men and women. None of them knows how to fight. We need fighters to train and lead them, and my role is to find these people, if you give me your blessing."

"Forgive me, Ali. The joy blinded me. You have my blessing, but be cautious, don't underestimate the emperor and his generals".

Chapter 2

Nine soldiers rode towards the emperor's castle in an ecstatic state of mind. They were eager to arrive at their destination because an unusual celebration was about to occur, the emperor's new son had been born. They spent three days deploying a security plan against any potential attack from the enemy. The soldiers carried the rank of commanders, which was the highest in the empire.

"Sometimes, I wonder if these precautions against the rebels are necessary!" asked one of the commanders.

His companions all agreed that the emperor and his advisors were exaggerating, considering the castle had a prime position on the outskirts of the forest. Not once had the rebels succeeded in attacking the king. Besides, who would dare approach this broad woodland?

One could easily get lost among its giant pine trees that had grown so tall, their tops lined up to create a rooftop of leaves that blocked the sun, making navigation difficult. Those who knew the forest well, still took a day to cross it.

Barracks that held at least a hundred soldiers were placed every ten miles, and even those who managed to make it out of the forest alive would find a bridge one mile in length and fifty feet in width in their way – it led to the castle where there were two walled and gated entrances. If the enemy managed to pass the first gate, they would be trapped between the two walls and exposed to shooters and barrels filled with fish oil.

The commanders were making good progress through the undulating part of the forest. But as they crossed a fallen tree, a deafening howling came from the shadows. They doubted it was the wolves and wondered if another commander might be trying to mess with them, breaking into laughter.

One of the commanders shouted out, "Come and join us! We have a deer that needs more than nine to finish it."

There was no reply, yet they still didn't realize they might be in danger until a shadow appeared on top of the hill, his face covered with a black mask. The shadows' height and frame indicated this could not be a soldier.

One of the commanders shouted, "Thin and short, that's not a soldier…" but before completing his sentence, an arrow pierced his neck.

Another commander screamed, "It's a trap, take your shields and protect yourselves."

The warning came too late for the three of them as they fell to death with arrows piercing their bodies. The five remaining used their shields to protect themselves, but no additional arrows came. They expected the attacker to run away, but he did not. His green eyes were the only thing they could see of the attackers' faces, as he was staring at them.

The commanders were edging toward the masked figure using their shields, while their attacker stood, ignoring all their threats. A moment before the clash, the masked fighter threw his bow to the ground, encouraging the commanders to dispose of their shields and sprint toward him.

But the intruder was quicker and retrieved two daggers from his boots and hurled them. Two more soldiers went down with wounds on their chests.

Rolling to the right to avoid the remaining three soldiers, the intruder retrieved two swords and went toward them. He used one blade to immobilize one of the remaining three soldiers and the other to cut off the foot of another.

Gathering all his strength, the last of the nine soldiers extended his sword, intending to cut the attacker in half. The intruder was quick though, taking a kneeling position and having retrieved the first sword, defended himself, causing the soldier to miss his target. The commander was exposed. As he attempted to turn, the blade cut him from behind.

The shadowed fighter went toward the injured man, who was sure of his death. The commander, in his desperation, threatened the intruder: "You'll be cut into pieces. No man dares to enter the property of the emperor and stay alive".

The attacker decided to reveal himself, taking off his hood, "But I'm not a man." Then proceeded to slaughter him like a sheep.

Indeed, she wasn't a man, but a beautiful young woman, with long brown curly hair and pale skin. Her green eyes were full of tears. She could no longer hold them in as they flowed down her cheek. On the one hand, she was delighted because she'd been planning this attack for years. On the other hand, she remembered a tragedy from her past. She should have been sitting next to her father as the princess of Token. Instead, she was forced to live in the shadows.

The woman let out a piercing scream.

Nora was her name. She was born twenty-one years ago in one of the most powerful kingdoms on earth, Token. She was the youngest and the only girl. Her father raised her like her brothers, trained her like a knight, and educated her to rule.

Her mother, the queen, was a daughter of a Speaker: a title given to men who devoted their whole life to knowledge. She taught her daughter their wisdom. The king made sure his older son, the heir, has an advisor like her – a strong and brave girl with a sharp mind. However, his enemy, the emperor, was working behind the scenes, turning the kingdom upside down and ruining its future.

Nora couldn't remember the details, but the memory of her father and brothers being taken to the execution yard never left her. She was strong enough to watch a bald soldier raise his giant sword and cut off their heads. She didn't scream, and neither did she cry.

Things didn't stop there. Nora found her mother hanging in her room. The princess was the only member of the royal family left, and the instructions from the emperor were clear: to wipe out the king's family.

Nora was fifteen years old at the time, devastated at her loss and knowing she would follow her family to her death. Ten soldiers took her out of the castle to execute her during the night. She was shaken with rage and terror.

What she didn't know, though, was that a masked knight lay in wait, unbeknownst to the soldiers. When he appeared out of the dark, she'd never seen a man like him and even doubted if he was human. He was quick and decisive, killing them all before unchaining her.

He spoke without taking off his mask, "You're the only heir of Token. Stay alive."

He had given Nora a bow, some arrows, and a beautiful dagger. Its curved blade had a golden pommel engraved with a circle and three vertical lines.

"Thank you. I hope I can see you one day to return the favor," Nora said.

"You're a queen. You're meant to be served." The man replied, "If it is meant to be, we'll meet again." Then he left.

In the beginning, it wasn't easy for Nora to get used to the wildlife. With no servants and no access to food, she was forced to sleep in the open air with no bed or even a cover to warm her at night, but her survival instinct was strong. She lived in caves and learned how to hunt and hide, and after she acquired confidence, she decided to live for one purpose: revenge.

Years passed. She tracked all the Token's traitors and – one by one – slaughtered them like beasts. When she was about to kill the last one on her list-her uncle- he told her, "You think I'm your enemy? You're dumb like your father. We are just puppets of the emperor's hand."

Nora cut his throat, but his last words made sense to her. She took another oath to kill as many as possible in the Empire.

This was not as easy as she expected, though. Nora had to learn everything about this strong empire while facing danger every day, living in that cursed forest and expecting each day to be her last.

She managed to survive, which led to this day, standing among nine bodies of the highest-ranked soldiers. Nora felt pride in her achievement but knew it was just the beginning.

Nora wished she could take down the whole empire but knew that no force on earth could stand against such a power, and every time she had this feeling of disappointment, she remembered her mother and how hopeful she was. Her mother had once told her that the world connects good hearts together, and whenever a man or a woman initiates good deeds, an invisible force in the universe inspires other good hearts to do the same thing.

Only a few people believed in these sayings that came from the Speakers, but Nora was raised as a princess; in other words, she was meant to rule the kingdom along with her brothers. Her father educated her not to believe in what the Speakers said, and now, while she was looking at the nine cadavers she took down, she wished her mother had been right. It would have shaken the Empire if other men and women were chasing their soldiers.

But her mother had an innocent heart that prevented her from seeing how cruel their world was. The Token princess considered that men were cowards and women weak.

It seemed that Nora's mother wasn't wrong, as on the other side of the forest, another rebel was about to mimic what she had just done, but with a move much bolder than hers.

The rebel was a tall man, muscular and robust. He had a thick beard, long hair, and brown eyes, which hid his grudges against the empire. Arsalan was his name; he dared to enter the forest, attacking from the south side , which he thought was an efficient tactic. By setting traps that never missed and after killing each soldier, he made sure that they were buried in order not to draw attention to himself. Before the Empire had a chance to realize that their count had been reduced, he did something that would turn them upside down.

He burnt one of the barracks which held more than eighty soldiers inside. He knew this would not be something he could hide and would get the emperor's attention.

Arsalan wanted to take down more barracks, but he was sure the emperor would stop at nothing to find the man who dared to burn down his barrack.

So Arsalan hid away. Not for long – certainly not forever – but until the emperor was off his scent, so he could resume bringing chaos.

Nevertheless , the revolution didn't stop at Nora and Arsalan. There were more than two rebels.

Chapter 3

If the emperor Ceres hadn't been raised by the wisest men on Earth – the Speakers – he may have let his rage destroy all the kingdoms. Instead, he sat in his council, his wrath simmering in his blood.

The Speakers taught Ceres many secrets, and one of them was that when he faced many enemies, he must know who he should stop first instead of attacking them all at once. Although the rebels' attacks shook the whole empire, he knew there was another enemy more dangerous; his anger. He was aware of how blinding it could be. The Speakers told him many stories about powerful men who lost everything, by forsaking wisdom for anger.

Upon delivering the rebels' news, he spoke to no one and decided to isolate himself for two days in his secret chamber, known only by his most trusted advisors.

After a night of thinking, Ceres realized that one of his weapons had started slipping out of his control; the terror he'd been spreading in the seven kingdoms for decades. Although he was short and not very strong, he'd always had a charisma that terrorized his enemies. Even the Speakers couldn't tell what it was about him: maybe his big blue eyes, the way he spoke, or his history. But in the wake of the rebel's attacks, Ceres felt his lethal weapon slipping from his grasp.

After two days of self-reflection, he decided to summon the council's eleven members. He called them "the generals." They had no idea what the meeting was about , except for the military chief, who had said farewell to his family. After what the rebels did, he assumed the emperor would hold him responsible and execute him.

Ceres was sitting with an emotionless look on his face. Each General went next to his chair and waited for their emperor to invite them to sit, but he didn't; he instead retrieved his sword and addressed a look to the military chief, who understood the untold command. He walked toward his emperor and knelt before him. Ceres decided to speak first, "Lord Peter, give me one good reason not to kill you."

Peter replied without raising his head, "There isn't, your highness. Hundreds of our soldiers died in their own land, and as your military chief, I take full responsibility."

The emperor kept his sword in his fist. Peter's voice shook as he continued, "Your highness, the stabilization you have provided us in the last decade is a blessing, but I wasn't wise enough to maintain it. Without danger, the soldiers slacked and underestimated our enemies."

The emperor put his sword in its sheath and ordered Peter to go to his chair. Then, he said, "A man who acknowledges his mistake deserves a second chance."

"Your highness, I will never fail you again"

Ceres gritted his teeth, "You'd better not, because I never give a third chance" He paused, "You may take your seats."

Although the emperor spread terror in all the seven kingdoms, when it came to his people –especially the close ones – he cared like they were family. He knew with certainty that they were a weapon against his enemy, and the emperor summoned them not just to place the blame, but to find a solution against the rebels.

Lord Peter cleared his throat. "I have some good news, your highness. We have captured Isaac. This is a letter I received this morning!"

Ceres opened the letter and stared at it for a while, then replied, "Well done Lord Peter, craftsmen are worse than rebels, we shall not let anyone live unless they bend the knee."

Peter was relieved to hear a compliment from his emperor and continued, "About the rebels, your highness, the attacks started about three months ago when the prince was born; ten soldiers and a leader were killed brutally, and we didn't find King Eleah. Then when we found nine commanders killed in the south of the forest, we turned the place upside down, but we found nothing except our soldiers' corpses . It didn't stop there, as four attacks followed, and each one had a different signature."

Ceres turned his face to his closest General, Ramessess, asking for his opinion.

"Your highness, I'm afraid this is one man's doing. He changed the way he attacked every time to spread fear among soldiers," explained the prime advisor and continued, "And it's definitely not the deposed king."

Peter guffawed. "Forgive me, Lord Ramessess, how can one man take over four hundred soldiers? Many among them were leaders and even commanders?"

"Setting traps!" replied the prime advisor.

"I'm afraid Lord Ramessess might be right; maybe he's trying to make us think he's not alone," corrected Ceres.

Peter couldn't disagree; instead, he suggested a solution. He had been hesitating for days, but not anymore. "Your highness, my lords. Last week, a soldier with a high rank came to me and volunteered to catch the rebels. I can say he's the most suitable man for such a mission."

The generals went furious and objected, except Ramessess, who stood and stared at them. "We'd better give Lord Peter a chance to explain his plan."

The treasury chief jumped, "This is a matter that shakes the whole empire, and you're suggesting assigning a soldier to such a mission!"

Peter didn't seem offended, he instead smiled, "You're right, Lord Philip, this might sound insane, but he's no ordinary soldier; you all know him. He's the previous gladiator, Ila."

All the generals looked at each other in a state of surprise, as this name was known throughout the whole empire. The ultimate gladiator, he first showed up in the Arena at the age of fifteen: no man could stand against him. He even once accepted a challenge from ten gladiators, and took them all down.

Ila was freed by his owner, Lady Bianca, before she passed. It had been a thank-you for the fortune he had brought her. After that, he chose to join the army, and it took him five years to climb six ranks and become a leader.

Peter knew he had got the emperor's attention when he commanded the guards to bring Ila at once. Ceres couldn't hide his eagerness to meet this champion. He had heard many stories about him, but they never spoke directly.

Ila finally showed up. Striding in a straight line, with wide steps, his hands moved in perfect harmony with his feet. Some of the generals hadn't seen him in years – since his old days in the Arena – and he looked different now with longer hair and a beard that was black with a few gray hairs. One of the servant girls who was preparing the drinks got distracted when she saw him, as a result, she poured a few drops on the carpet. She remembered seeing him in the arena half-naked with a barrel chest, and a very well-developed stomach muscles. His brown eyes went with the leather suit he was wearing and before reaching the first chair, he stopped and knelt. He didn't stand until his chief, Peter asked him to; he went closer to the emperor and bowed again.

"You don't have to do it twice in my council. State your name, soldier," said the emperor.

Ila stood and lowered his head. "Forgive me, your highness, I have never addressed a man in your position before. I'm your humble servant, Ila."

"You claimed that you could capture the rebels when hundreds of soldiers, led by experienced commanders, failed to do so. Don't you see that your claim is insulting to your chief and the whole empire?"

"It is your highness. I don't mean to doubt our army, but as I mentioned to my chief before – if I can't catch the rebel scum, then you can have my life instead," replied Ila.

Ramessess berated, "And what good can your life do to us?"

"Nothing my lord, but to me, it's everything. As a leader in the army, I have a great life thanks to the generosity of our empire, so why would I risk losing my life?" replied Ila.

The emperor liked how Ila answered the question and understood why Peter entrusted him with such a mission, so he decided to ask him if he had any plan.

Ila enthusiastically nodded, but Ramessess jumped in before he could speak. "You have a better plan than your chief?"

"My chief has responsibility for an empire and seven kingdoms, so he handled every problem with a military approach," explained Ila, "Plus, I'm a soldier in his army. My success belongs to him and the empire."

Ramessess smiled and exchanged a look with Peter, who asked Ila to walk them through his plan.

Ila raised his head and turned it slowly, trying to make eye contact with each one. "I once met a Speaker, and I was lucky to spend three nights with him. His wisdom made me realize that our world has a lot of secrets that most men miss. One of them is when there's a problem we're unable to solve, it is not wise to keep trying the same methods over and over again. Rather, we need to change our angle, and that's what has happened with the rebels. Although we have the strongest army in the world, and we control the seven kingdoms, we couldn't even identify them. I think we need to think like rebels and not like soldiers,"

Ramessess loved what Ila had just said, but he always chose to be tough on people, so he could distinguish a talker from a doer. "And how do you intend to do that, Ila?"

Ila smiled. "First step: know your enemy. In this case, there are many."

Another general didn't hesitate to intervene, "We all concluded that was a one man's doing, while you are implying that there are many!"

Ila replied, "My lord, with all due respect, this is what I call thinking as a soldier. You assume a rebel is as rational as you, but I can assure you he's not. He is not interested in results; he only cares about showing off his strength."

The general mocked Ila, "I don't see the point!"

"My lord, my point is; if he was one man, he would've wanted us to know that. It would make him look stronger!" replied Ila.

A general grimaced, "This is nonsense."

Ila smiled, "I won't disagree with you, my lord. After all, this is just my opinion, but I went further and examined the bodies with the healers before burying them. Many weapons were used to kill the soldiers: spears, swords, axes, and arrows. In addition, some sword cuts suggested that the killer was left-handed and others right-handed. After days of research, I believe there are up to six rebels."

They were all petrified, saying nothing except staring at Ila, who cleared his throat and started explaining. "Nora, the daughter of the previous king of Token, tracks the big fish – the commanders. She is an excellent shooter and a fierce warrior.

"Arsalan, an ex-commander in the Kingdom of Toprak: fire and axe are his ultimate weapons.

"Alighieri, a farmer in the Kingdom Solum, uses swords like his own hand. He attacks outside the forest and knows how to be unpredictable. Though he never kills, he prefers stealing from soldiers and humiliating them.

"Keita. He was brought from the Kingdom of Grond to be a gladiator here in the empire, but he succeeded to run away. He's the boldest among them; his attacks were always next to the castle's bridge.

"Last but not least, Sai from Dharatee and Roulan from Turang, two lovers who decided to run away from their kingdoms when they were forbidden to get married. They fooled our guards and pretended to be Speakers, poisoning 147 soldiers."

The emperor kept looking at Ila and couldn't hide his admiration.

"Your highness, they don't know each other, but they all share one common goal: revenge. But mark my words, I will catch them."

Ceres stood and ordered everyone to leave the council except for Ila.

The generals were surprised by the emperor's act. For the first time in their life, they saw Ceres behaving in a way that suggested he was worried. Most felt like he was overreacting.

Ceres was face to face with Ila. He hadn't seen any results yet, but his gut never failed him; he could see the greatness of this man, so he wanted to make sure that this leader would serve him for the rest of his life.

"I can tell that you will fulfill your promise," "What is the greatest thing you want to achieve in your life?"

Ila's eyes were filled with tears, and he said all that mattered to him was serving his empire and becoming a commander one day.

"Even a general's position wouldn't suit a man like you!" said Ceres, "There are five families in our empire who were meant to be served; Wud, Sua, Yagut, Yowk, and Nasr. These families are the Gods' descendants. Therefore, they are the ones with clean blood, and I promise, if you fulfill this mission, you'll become a member of one of these families," explained the emperor.

"Forgive me your highness, but how can I be part of these holy families when I don't have their blood?"

Ceres unsheathed his sword. Ila had never seen such beauty, its shining blade and golden pommel left him speechless.

"This is the Majesty. It has been in our families since the creation of the earth – its steel was made by the Gods' blood." Ceres could see the confusion in Ila's eyes, and continued, "All you need to do to become one of us, is take a dirty blood's life with the Majesty"

Ila didn't find the words to express his gratitude, but he dared to ask, "Thank you for your generosity, your highness. You must care greatly about the demise of rebels to give such a gift."

"I've spent years with the Speakers. I've learned many valuable things. One of them is that the strongest enemy is not the one with the biggest army," sighed Ceres, " but the enemy with no fear . What these bastard rebels did was bold, and to me, they are like a flame. They might look weak compared to our empire, but if we don't shut them down now, they will grow and burn us all."

Chapter 4

Ila's first command was to stop chasing the rebels; the soldiers received orders to return to their routine and forget about the insurgents. Most of them did so obediently who wanted to fight the rebels? when many of their comrades had died doing it? But others disagreed and considered it an act of cowardice; they wanted badly to catch these rebels who murdered their loved ones, but they couldn't do anything about it. Even the generals disagreed initially, but Ila persuaded them, and they all acknowledged his excellent tactic.

Ila was an intelligent man, and his outstanding skills didn't prevent him from respecting his adversaries; he was aware that what the six rebels did was strategically brilliant, so he chose to think like them: What would I do next if I were in their shoes?

The answer was evident. They would hide until the emperor's rage went off, so he decided to be unpredictable and give the rebels a false impression.

After a month, Ila's plan worked, and the first to catch the bait were Sai and Roulan. Their last attack gave them the courage to play a more prominent role, and they decided to eliminate a general; the one who was responsible for the conflicts between their two kingdoms.

Sai used to be a thief, spending his entire childhood in the alleys of Dharatee, stealing to survive. He once dared to steal a dagger from a Turangy general and got away with it, or so he thought – until a girl had cornered him.

She had pushed the back of her forearm against his neck. "Is that how you welcome your guests?"

Sai had been scared and tried to resist, but the highborn seemed very strong, so he chose the peaceful way. "It's in my right pocket. Please take it and let me go."

"Not so fast, your place is in prison!" replied the girl and commanded him to walk.

"Please don't take me to the soldiers, I will lose my life there."

"And you didn't think about that before stealing from a general? Move!"

Sai didn't obey and exploded in her face. "You think I enjoy what I do? I have no family, no friends; if I don't steal, I die!"

It didn't work on her, she considered his justifications as excuses to do what he loved to do, but he didn't give up. "You think I fell from the sky as a thief while you burst from the soil as a noble girl? There are circumstances that made each one of us who we are."

She didn't reply, and he wanted to continue but couldn't, lowering his head without another word.

The Turangy lady guessed why he couldn't look at her. A man usually did that when his tears decided to fall from his eyes, and she knew that men could lie using words, but their eyes rarely do.

The girl crossed her arms and kept staring at him.

"My parents taught me that stealing is wrong, and they were right, but our standards change when we face starvation," said Sai.

"You want to tell me that your only motive for stealing is food?"

"Well, I wish I could afford other things by stealing," replied Sai.

The highborn girl opened her lips slightly, letting her white and perfectly shaped teeth smile, "Like what?"

"Buying some beautiful clothes. That way, I might convince a highborn girl like you to marry me." The girl smiled again and kept staring at him, "I have everything a girl like you could wish for, except a good appearance!"

Somehow his words found a place in her heart, so she decided not only to forgive him but also to hand him a bag. "Here are ten silver coins. How much time could you live on that without stealing?"

Sai was perplexed and couldn't believe his eyes. He knelt before her and informed her that he could use this money to live for months, if not a year.

"Fine, I'll send you another ten coins in three months. I have eyes in your kingdom. If you steal once more, I will kill you myself."

He smiled at her and asked, "What is your name? No one has ever treated me like you did, and I want to remember you."

"Roulan," replied the girl.

After three months, Roulan kept her word and sent him silver with her servant. But to her surprise, the servant returned with the silver, plus a flask and a parchment. Roulan opened the letter first and started reading.

"Dear Roulan,

My father once told me that what determines good people is the ability to change themselves from bad to good, but changing someone else is what makes them exceptional. You're one of those exceptions. Thanks to you, I'm a different man.

I felt embarrassed the day you arrested me, and the silver you gave me made me realize that there are still nice people in our world. Instead of spending what you gave me on food, I took a risk and used it to buy tools to re-launch my father's business, which was making perfumes. He taught me before he passed, and my business is working now. I'm making my living thanks to you, and you were right; I wasn't a victim.

As a thank you, I collected the best flowers and made a perfume for you that has never been worn, not even by the queen herself."

She took the flask and opened it, and when she smelled it, it was so fragrant that she couldn't take her nose out of it. The thief wasn't exaggerating, as she had never smelled something as beautiful as this perfume.

Roulan was relieved to learn that she made a difference in someone's life, but also shocked to know a man with such talent could have been living on the streets – so she decided to pay him a visit. To her surprise, he was a different person. She found him extremely attractive even though she didn't like his new haircut, with the sides sheared close to the skin. Talking with him made her forget all the crises and tragedies she'd been through, and she kept seeing him until she knew that he was the man she meant to spend her life with.

When her father refused their marriage, she decided to marry Sai anyway and they ran away together. They went to a village and lived there for years, but the Unionists didn't let anyone live in peace. They butchered everyone in their village, including their four years old son, so their quest for vengeance began.

After succeeding in entering the empire's castle and poisoning over a hundred soldiers, their second plan of attack was bolder. They wanted to enter the castle as Speakers. Sai would use his sneaking skills to enter the general's chamber and slip poison into one of his jars. As for Roulan, she had insisted on coming along. They argued about it, but she was too stubborn to listen.

Sai and Roulan dressed up as Speakers, wearing white robes with hoods. Each one held a long stick in their left hand and pulled a mule with another.

Before reaching the gate, four guards approached them, and one of them removed his helmet and knelt.

"Forgive me, your honor, but we're experiencing some security issues and must verify the identity of every visitor."

Roulan couldn't speak behind her hood, as the Speakers were always male, so Sai had no choice but to raise his tone, "How dare you, soldiers! We're no ordinary visitors. We are the Speakers."

Ila came from behind and spoke, "I'm sorry, your honor, but it is a necessary evil," Ila added, "Though I have to say, your tone surprises me, as raising your voice is a sin in the Speakers' belief."

Roulan couldn't wait longer and took off her robe with a sword in her hands, cutting one of the guards' throats. Before engaging with the second one, she heard, "Another step, and he'll die."

She turned and saw Ila putting a sword on Sai's neck, whose eyes weakened her and made her release her weapon. They chained her, along with her husband.

"I promised his highness to bring them all at once, so put them in a cage in the forest until we bring the other rebels," ordered Ila.

The third rebel to be spotted in the forest was Keita; a man most soldiers feared, given his history in the Arena when he was a gladiator.

Keita set a trap next to the bridge and was waiting for his victims to show up. When they did –six soldiers singing merrily on their way to the castle – he launched at them, But a cord hidden among the fallen leaves pulled him from his left foot, and the next thing he heard a burst of laughter from the soldiers and insults about his skin.

Keita was hanging upside down, thinking about what would happen next, and the only options left were whether die or return to slavery. He couldn't let either happen.

Suddenly the laughter of the soldiers stopped when they saw their prisoner stretching his giant body until his hands reached upwards to his feet. He then retrieved a dagger from his boot and cut the cord to fall on the ground. In no time, he killed all six of them. But before he could relish his victory, twenty soldiers showed up from the trees, with arrows ready to shoot.

The soldiers spent the night drinking strawberry juice to celebrate catching the three rebels, but not Ila. He was too concerned about catching the remaining ones – more specifically Alighieri, a farmer from the Kingdom Solum: a fierce knight, with a sharp mind, and hard to outsmart.

Ila chose to take a risk and went alone to Alighieri's trap, willing to challenge him in combat.

Alighieri was hiding behind a rock, waiting for his prey to show up. Surprisingly, there was only one soldier. The Solumy knew that the brown suit in the empire was given to the leaders. He appeared from behind the rock and walked towards his prisoner with his bow, ready to release the arrow.

"The minute I release this arrow, you will leave this world!" said Alighieri.

"I was told you're not a killer!" replied Ila.

Alighieri pulled the bowstring at its maximum and aimed for his adversary's chest, "Sometimes we don't have a choice."

Ila didn't show the slightest fear and surprised his enemy by inviting him to a challenge.

Alighieri lowered his bow and replied, "I'm the one with the arrow. Why in hell would I fight you?"

Ila wasn't surprised by his opponent's intelligence. "I might not be smart, but I'm a reasonable man. Only a fool would come alone to your trap, given your reputation." Alighieri didn't reply, and Ila continued, "I caught three rebels sharing the same cause as you, they are in the small barrack of the south. If you win, you'll have a chance to release them!"

Alighieri had heard about the other insurgents who had turned the empire upside down, and he yearned to team up with fighters who shared the same cause as him. It was like a dream.

Initially, he hesitated, thinking that his enemy might be fooling him, but he decided to take the risk and humiliate this arrogant soldier.

Alighieri fetched his sword and sprinted toward Ila, who knelt and caught his opponent's hand, rolling him over. His body smashed onto the ground. Before the Solumy got up, Ila put his feet on Alighieri's right hand, blocking his sword, and then retrieved a dagger, and put it on his throat, leaving him no choice but to surrender.

After Alighieri's capture, the two remaining rebels were the toughest ones to catch – but Ila knew they were the ones with the softest hearts. He captured two children, one was Nora's cousin, and the other a Topraky girl. Nora couldn't risk her eight-year-old cousin's life, and she surrendered. Even Arsalan didn't need a lot of convincing: the minute he recognized that the little girl was Topraky, he fell on his knees and surrendered.

Ila had fulfilled the mission he'd been planning for weeks. The six rebels were put in a horse cart with a cage. They were all angry and disappointed, and the tension was high. Nora gave a fierce look to Arsalan, "It's because of you, Toprakies, that the empire got stronger."

Roulan knew her accent and decided to respond, "Shut up, Token, you're the poison Ceres used to ruin our kingdoms."

Nora addressed an angry look to Roulan, who stood and yelled at her. But Keita intervened before a fight could break out, "Don't you think that this is what made the empire stronger; setting conflicts among our kingdoms?"

"It's like you're from heaven. You Grondies also had a hand in this," said Arsalan.

"No, Grond isn't responsible; neither is Solum nor any other kingdom. Without Grond, we wouldn't be able to decorate our robes and women's necks with precious stones. Without Solum, we'd still be living in tents.

Toprakies made our life more beautiful with their skills in fabric. It's also the case for Turang, Dharatee, and Turba. Each one of these nations made the world a better place, and those from our races who helped the empire to gain power and enslave us are outlaws. They're not from our kingdoms. They're from the Kingdom of the devil."

No one said a word, and Keita continued, "Our ancestors lived in peace until the empire came and divided us. And like they say: the enemy of my enemy is my friend. I suggest that we stick together and forget about our internal conflicts."

A voice came from behind and said, "I didn't know that people with dark skin could be so wise."

Keita turned and saw their capturer Ila, "Like you chose your skin!"

Ila advanced to the cage and said, "I didn't choose my skin, but it chose me for a reason – to enslave all of you."

Keita ignored Ila but deep down, he was devastated. He wished his rebellion could have gone further and taken more soldiers from the empire, but he knew that his time had come.

He wasn't worried about the torture that would precede his execution, but he was rather sad to leave the world of living without seeing a glimpse of the empire's defeat.

Keita looked around him and saw people with eyes full of sorrow and anger and spoke again. "My name is Keita. No doubt you all hate the empire. I'll be honored to die among friends like you."

None of them replied, but he didn't give up. "When I was ten years old, I was taken away from my family and offered as a present to a wealthy house in the empire.

They wanted me to be their gladiator, and when I insisted on them to take me home, they brought me my mother's head instead."

A tear dropped from his eyes, and he could hardly speak. Alighieri tapped on his knee to calm him down, but he continued, "I ended up doing what they asked me, which was killing people who I didn't know, and when I decided to stop, they tortured and sentenced me to die."

Alighieri interjected, "How did you survive?"

Keita's eyes lit up. "I don't know. One night, I was in a dungeon bleeding and expecting to be executed, and the next day, I found myself out of the empire, free as a bird. Someone has helped me."

"That's almost what happened to me. I didn't even see who did that!" replied Alighieri.

Nora wondered if it was the same person who rescued her five years ago, but she kept this nice memory to herself. She added, "You know what, I don't care if I die! I'm proud of myself for taking nine of their soldiers alone."

Arsalan addressed her with a look of mockery, and she added, "They were commanders."

There was a peal of laughter filling the cage. They forgot about their capture and exchanged their stories without thinking about what would happen next.

CHAPTER 5

Long before the empire was founded, the world was in a state of an endless war, and each ethnicity was trying to wipe off the other. The weak kingdoms fell quickly, and only seven remained. One of them changed the course of history thanks to a king. Tamim was his name.

He was able to strengthen his kingdom, Turba, until it became the most powerful realm. They were the wealthiest in the world, and no army could resist them, but against all odds, they did not cleanse races like the other kings were trying to. Tamim did something bold enough to shake all the kingdoms including his: a truce proposition that was rejected categorically, even by his advisors.

Tamim proved them wrong, though, and persuaded each king by showing them that wars wouldn't stop until humanity ceased to exist and that the world was too big to have one nation. He made them realize that their interest lays on accepting his proposition. All they needed to do was swear allegiance to him.

They agreed that whoever initiated an attack, the six other kingdoms would have the right to unite against the attackers.

The commoners from each race resisted this change and refused any form of alliance with each other. Still, the removal of borders attracted most merchants to explore the other kingdoms, proposing their goods to the people who couldn't help themselves when they saw things they had never seen in their lives.

The commercial interest connected people on many levels, helping them to see how beautiful other kingdoms were.

At the time of war, the kings' focus was limited to the military, and they weren't wrong. Preparing for battles was a key element to staying alive. But peace opened their eyes to improving the quality of their buildings, to protect people from the heat of summer and the cold of winter. Farming was also an area that was revolutionized.

Kingdoms made deals of exchanging seeds and farmers to enrich their lands and stand against famine. The same thing went for healthcare, hoping to fight diseases and ease the labor for women with children.

Things went even further when the kingdoms started forming alliances with each other through marriages. Obviously, this didn't please those with an interest in wars. A group of blacksmiths' whose businesses were shut down because of the new system adopted by the kings. They were meeting secretly, trying to set conflicts between kingdoms by killing civilians using arrows with a mark of another realm. It would have worked if it weren't for Tamim, who shut down their plan, and the age of war went down in history or so people thought.

No one was aware of the outlaws hidden in the mountains; they didn't commit any crimes, and the title was given to them for the crimes of their ancestors hundreds of years ago. They refused to bend the knee to any king.

They were a few thousand people who chose to live far from the seven kingdoms and preferred to live a simple life on warm lands the whole year, so tents were enough to shelter them. They earned their living through farming and hunting. They also had the skill of extracting precious stones from mines, but they didn't know their value at the time. They were great fighters. Whether a girl or a boy, they started learning how to fight at an early age.

The outlaws were happy with their lives as long as they were no longer chased by the seven kingdoms and had access to all their needs. But things had changed since a new leader took over the tribe. His ambition was higher than anyone before him. He wanted to establish an eighth kingdom.

Initially, his people thought he was insane, but he convinced them of his plan by bringing some Speakers. They told them the history of many famous kingdoms, which were founded by a few people. The outlaws' thirst for vengeance raised their motivation to stand with their new leader in his first quest.

First, he infiltrated the kingdoms, pretending to be a merchant so he could learn everything about them. The few months he spent there helped him to see how the people were addicted to gold and silver, especially those holding power, so he decided to take advantage of the precious stones he possessed and succeeded in becoming a wealthy man.

With his social skills, he made powerful friends by spoiling them with gold. In exchange, they helped him build a walled city for his people and called it the eighth kingdom. He was aware that his small kingdom wasn't strong enough to destroy all of his enemies, so his attacks were secretly organized and done mainly on civilians.

In the meantime, he was focusing on something that would shift the power to his kingdom; it was the preparation of the heir, his son Ceres who had an exceptional education. Ceres was entrusted to people called the Speakers; they were extraordinary men, who dedicated their whole life to knowledge and thinking, and his son spent all of his childhood under their care, learning everything they knew. His father brought him back to the castle when he was twelve and provided him with the right learning for a king. When he was nineteen, the king died, and Ceres took over his father's legacy.

Ceres had a sharp mind, like his father. Still, the seven years he'd spent with the Speakers taught him many secrets. One of them was, "If you want a different result, you need to try different methods," so instead of war with swords and catapults, he decided to use his wealth to weaken his enemies.

Ceres sent some of his men – pretending to be merchants – on a special mission. They called themselves the Facilitators; they lent money with slight interest.

Ceres' idea wasn't to make profits, rather seize the possession of the clients unable to pay back. He targeted council's members and noble families, and his plan worked. He gained a lot of power throughout the possessions he ceased, and along with his wealth, he was able to control all the remaining kingdoms without losing any man from his people. Of course not through ruling them, instead placing new kings from their race who answered to him.

Thousands of people left the seven kingdoms and joined the new realm for the sake of wealth, making the new king Ceres more powerful.

Ceres decided to have a new name for his kingdom. He chose the 'empire' instead of a kingdom and gave it the name of the Union. This name was meant to make people believe that Ceres saw them as equal and his intentions were to unite them.

Chapter 6

Isaac was no ordinary man. For starters, he was one of the few people to have blood from two kingdoms. His mother was a Topraki princess, and his father was a prime advisor of Solum.

Isaac never liked swords or politics. His only interest was in tools, and he wanted to learn everything, from forging weapons to building castles. His father disapproved and wanted him to learn politics so that one day, he could sit alongside the king.

Luckily, his mother took him behind his father's back to learn from some craftsmen and his learning curve was incredibly fast. He didn't stop at one master or two. He learned from all those in his kingdom, and at the age of sixteen, his father could no longer prevent him and gave him his blessing to see other masters in the other realms.

The skills he acquired, and his mindset allowed him to revolutionize many industries. Sadly, things got tighter when the Union empire took power. His father decided to hide him when he learned about the emperor's intention: killing every craftsman or scientist in the seven kingdoms. Ceres went mad when he learned about the existence of Isaac, who was described as a legendary craftsman and scientist. He had Isaac's parents tortured until they lost their lives. Isaac couldn't hide for long and got caught by the emperor's soldiers.

The mastermind preferred to die a thousand times than serve the emperor. He knew that Ceres' ambition had no limit, and it wouldn't stop until the seven kingdoms were wiped out. Isaac was aware of his skills and how dangerous they could be, and he could guess why the emperor summoned him. It was not for making new horse carts or a fancy bed but rather for something more dangerous, and Isaac chose to die instead.

Isaac assumed that he would be given a chamber in the castle with food and servants, but he was mistaken. The soldiers pulled him into a cell and locked him in there with no food. He panicked in the beginning until he realized it was just a game the emperor was playing to scare him.

Isaac was tired enough not to feel hungry and didn't wake up until a soldier opened the cell, pulled him by his arms, and took him to the emperor.

When he got to the council, he was so scared. It was broad; the walls were painted brown, and dozens of white sculptures were on every corner . At the center, a beardless man was sitting on his throne. His eyes were blue. On each side, there were chairs occupied by men wearing suede robes in different colors. They were all staring at the mastermind; he felt scared but decided to hide his emotions and advanced toward his enemy. For the first time in his life, Isaac regretted not following his father's advice to be a fighter. He wished he could kill the emperor, then realized that even a champion gladiator couldn't do that with the protection Ceres had.

"The mastermind in the flesh," said Ceres.

Isaac chose not to respond, and Ceres added, "And he looked brave. Do you know at least why you're here"?

Isaac could no longer ignore the emperor, so he growled, "I'd rather die a thousand times than join an evil man like you."

The emperor laughed, "Poor boy, you think you're here to be begged to join us? Oh no, I would never allow dirty blood in my empire!"

"You think I don't know your games?" accused Isaac.

Ceres stood and shouted, "You think because you learned how to use some tools, I'd beg you to join me? I have the smartest craftsmen in the world."

Isaac was convinced that Ceres was bluffing. Otherwise, why would he bother to receive him in the council?

Ceres walked towards him, put his hand on his shoulder, and then addressed him in a firm tone. "Here's the thing, I could use a man like you in my empire, but I won't take that risk. I must admit that any kingdom could reverse the balance with men like you, so I wanted to cut this hope and kill you. Someone very special to me will handle your execution, after a long torture."

Now things got clearer to Isaac. The emperor was smart enough to know that the seven kingdoms' hopes lay on men like Isaac. He was not only tracking them but executing them publicly to spread fear in those who were attempting to become like them one day. And Isaac's assumption was correct, as the emperor ordered the guards to take him back to his cell.

Ceres' state of mind didn't make him forget about the rebels, "Lord Peter, do you want me to go and pursue the rebels myself? It's been weeks since Ila went chasing them. Have you had any news?"

"I'm afraid not, your highness, but I know how critical this matter is to you. We should have good news very soon," replied Peter, "In the meantime, I'm enhancing the castle's security and I have added more barracks in the forest. I also ordered the guards to not let any Speaker inside the castle unless he reveals himself".

"Isn't that humiliating to men like the Speakers?" snapped Ceres.

Ramessess, the prime advisor, intervened this time, "Your Highness, I've spoken with the Highest Speaker, and he gave his blessing for this action. He said that the security of our empire comes first."

The emperor couldn't disagree or place blame, but he was disappointed with Ila. Ceres always considered himself an excellent judge of character. However, the delay of Ila indicated that he was not who he thought he was.

Before they were dismissed, a guard entered the room with no permission. Without an urgent matter, he could have lost his head for interrupting the council. He knelt before the emperor and didn't rise until he was asked to, "A soldier came with a message from Lord Ila, may I let him in?"

Ceres stood and shouted, "Bring him in!"

The soldier showed up with a wide smile on his face. The emperor didn't want to jump to any conclusion, so he commanded the soldier to speak.

"Your highness, I was with Lord Ila. The six rebels are in his custody. He sent me to inform you. He will bring them in the next three days at most," said the soldier.

The emperor stood and said with a wide smile, "Stand up, soldier! You will be rewarded a hundred gold coins for delivering such news. You are dismissed," ordered Ceres. Then addressed his generals with a question, "Now that we have captured these rats, how can I be sure this will never happen again?"

They all were thinking about enhancing the security in the castle and the forest, though such a response seemed obvious, and the emperor would have never asked such questions if it was the case.

The only one who dared to speak was Ramessess, "Your highness, our defense system is strong enough to hold an army, yet few individuals evaded us. Two of them dared to enter the castle and poisoned over a hundred soldiers,"

Hearing this wasn't pleasing to Ceres, so he asked in a firm tone, "Do you have a point, Lord Ramessess ?"

"Forgive me, my lord. But what I wanted to say is; these individuals were like phantoms. We knew nothing about them except the losses they caused us."-

Ceres said nothing, but Peter did. "Lord Ramessess , we just received the news that Ila captured them!"

"A few months ago, there was not a single rebel. Suddenly, six showed up and took over five hundred soldiers. There will be others if we don't act accordingly," explained Ramessess, as no one opened their mouths, so he continued, "It's the security of the seven kingdoms we should question, not ours."

The emperor finally understood Ramessess ' idea and loved it; the empire controlled the kings and generals in the seven kingdoms, but not the commoners. He realized that if rebels kept showing up, the risk would grow further.

Ceres decided to go to his secret chamber to organize his thoughts, so he could move forward into another stage that would repress every soul thinking to revolt against the empire.

Chapter 7

The six rebels were inside a small cage that could barely hold them, exhausted from one day on the road without a sip of water, not to mention the disappointment of being captured. Luckily some of them were strong enough to keep their optimism high; Nora was one of them, staring at Roulan and Sai trying to engage in a conversation. When Roulan smiled back, she asked her how she met her husband.

Sai jumped in, "I robbed her father, she then caught me and decided to free me. I made her a perfume and thanks to it she fell in love with me."

Nora looked surprised and asked, "You mean she fell in love with you first?"

Sai turned to his wife, who was just smiling, and asked Nora, "Why not?"

Nora realized she somehow offended him and didn't find any words, but Kieta did, "Have you ever looked at yourself in the mirror!"

The smile on Roulan's face disappeared, and her face turned red, but her husband held her hand, "My love, he's just joking!"

Nora couldn't let silence dominate and asked another question, "Who has something that could cheer us up?"

Keita was the first to volunteer, telling them a joke that made even Arsalan laugh. It was about a man standing on a bridge and screaming the word fifteen repeatedly until a curious man went to ask why he was screaming fifteen". Keita couldn't stop himself from laughing. Tears were dripping from his eyes, and he pulled himself together and mumbled, "Do you know what the screamer did?".

They had no clue, and Keita continued, "He threw the curious man off the bridge and screamed sixteen."

They all laughed hysterically, even Keita, But their laughter was cut short by Ila, who took Keita by surprise from behind, wrapping a belt around his neck. He kept squeezing until Keita was about to faint.

Ila released him and exclaimed, "I hope you can shut up now!"

Keita fell and kept coughing, while Alighieri helped him to breathe. The atmosphere turned dark. After a while, Sai looked at Keita and whispered, "Keita, look at me."

Keita ignored Sai, thinking that he was making fun of him.

"I said, look at me." Echoed Sai and redirected his sight next to Keita's feet.

Keita lowered his head and saw a nail. No one understood Sai's intention until he whispered, "I can use this nail to unlock our chains and the door."

Without questioning his credibility, Keita kicked the nail to him, and Sai used it to unlock his chains like it was a key. He did the same thing for all of them, and also opened the door, but before they got out Alighieri warned them, "Their leader Ila fights like a devil, at least three of us should attack him,"

"He's the devil himself," added Keita

Arsalan boasted, "Let me worry about him. Just make sure you two face the weak soldiers."

Alighieri nodded and hoped Arsalan wouldn't regret his arrogance.

When they launched from the cage, a soldier screamed. "They're running, they're running!"

Keita advanced toward him and said, "Not before giving you a present."

The soldier pulled his sword and ran towards the Grondy rebel, who avoided his hit by kneeling, then lifted him on his back and smashed him on a rock; the other soldiers attacked, but the six rebels took them all in a matter of minutes.

Alighieri felt lucky that their leader Ila wasn't there, and before they took horses to run, Ila appeared smiling and looking like he didn't care about all the fallen soldiers .

Arsalan touched Alighieri's shoulder and asked sarcastically, "Is this the devil you were talking about? I'm going to send him to hell."

Arsalan took a sword from one of the soldiers down and sprinted toward his enemy. Before the clash, Ila moved quickly to the left avoiding the hit of his opponent. Arsalan hesitated and before he could twist, a kick came to him from behind, followed by a punch in the back of the neck. He fell to the ground like his head was taken away.

The rest of the rebels decided to follow Alighieri's advice and attacked together, but they couldn't even touch Ila. He held Nora by her arm and threw her on Roulan. They both fell, and Ila quickly moved to the left avoiding Keita's hit, and kicked him from behind. Sai raised his sword, aiming for Ila's chest, but the Unionist was quick. He held Sai by his arm and threw him to the side.

Nora was down watching Ila beating them one by one, but she had a glimpse of hope when Alighieri was aiming for Ila's neck with his sword. Sadly the soldiers' leader was like a ghost holding Alighieri's wrist, rolling him over, and smashing him on a tree. They were all down, and Ila didn't even fetch his sword.

Keita was down next to Nora. He whispered to her, "Why didn't he kill us?"

She was holding her shoulder from the pain and seethed, "He's just a dog of the emperor. He was ordered to take us alive, but I'm not going to let that happen!"

Ila smiled. "You didn't change much, Nora. Still the same temper. Even the Speakers' power couldn't take it out of you."

Nora was surprised and didn't understand how this man was aware of her relationship with the Speakers.

Ila shocked them even more when he raised his hand and said, "I'm a friend!"

Nora seized the opportunity and went with her sword to Ila's neck, who didn't even blink. "I will send your head as a present to your pathetic emperor," she threatened.

"You have grown up since the last time I saw you," replied Ila.

Nora was eager to see the cut on his throat, but she was intrigued by the man who knew some of her past.

Ila kept his smile and replied, "You're a queen. You're meant to be served."

Nora lowered her sword and was in awe. When she regained her voice, she said, tears filling her eyes, "If it is meant to be, we'll meet one day."

Ila nodded and smiled.

The other five rebels had no idea what was happening. Nora threw her sword and turned to them, "This man is my hero; he's the one who gave me back life and hope with it."

Arsalan carried a sword and went toward them, "He's still one of Ceres' dogs, and he has to die!"

"Commander Arsalan, do you remember how you survived your execution?" replied Ila and continued, "Keita, no gladiator could survive an execution except you, you know why? And what about you, Sai and Roulan? Have you ever asked yourselves why the villagers agreed to host you?"

Alighieri interrupted him, "And I assume you're the one who pulled me from the river and cured my injuries,"

Ila smiled and nodded.

Arsalan spent three years thinking about the night before his execution, wondering who had left his cell unlocked. He assumed it was a clumsy soldier's mistake. Sai and Roulan naively thought that the villagers were friendly and accepted to host them for free, but now that this stranger reminded them of those moments with an explanation, they couldn't doubt he was behind it .

"I'm not here to remind you that you're in my debt. On the contrary, I'm here first to thank you for your remarkable work. The emperor can hardly sleep because of you," said Ila.

Nora looked at him and smiled, then asked him to tell them who he was.

"In the Union, I'm known as Ila. I was born in the Kingdom of Turba, and I'm here to form an alliance that our kings couldn't do," replied Ila and stopped for a while, then continued, "My real name is Ali."

Ali knew how hard his mission would be. The six people he wanted to gather carried a lot of hatred for each other, and each considered his or her nation to be the most decent one; although that idea wasn't something they were born with. Instead, it had been instilled in their minds. Even the wisest men couldn't trace the roots of this thinking.

Ali wished each of them could ask himself the following question, *"What did I do to become a Topraki, Grondy, Dharatee...?"* The answer would be "Nothing."

The Turban rebel wasn't surprised by the reaction of some of them, when Ali suggested working together. Arsalan was the first to object, "I owe you a lot, and you're a man I respect, but there's too much history between our kingdoms, and I prefer to work on my own."

Ali didn't reply and was thrilled to see Nora, the princess of Token, came next to him and said , "I'll go wherever you go, and I will be your companion on your quest until we take down the empire or die trying."

Keita also joined in and said, "I don't have a pretty face like Nora, and I don't know how to speak gently like a princess, but my life and sword are yours!"

Sai and Roulan chose not to stay either, and informed him of their return to the Kingdom of Turang to settle there.

"Thank you for the nail by the way. You could have killed Keita," Roulan said, winking.

"Is it true?" asked Keita angrily. Ali just smiled.

The remaining rebel Alighieri was very hesitant, and before Keita threw a joke on him, he said, "I can't stand living with a debt on my neck,"

Empire of Rebels: Rise of Rebels

While the three who chose not to join were preparing their horses, Ali went to speak with them, "I respect your choices, but remember, it's never too late to join us," he then handed them two parchments and said, "This is a map. If you're lost or you change your mind, go to the place circled in red,"

The three smiled at him and took their leave, although Ali wished they could be by his side. Deep down, he knew they would meet again. He turned to his three new companions, who were staring at him.

Nora asked enthusiastically, "What are we going to do?".

"What do you suggest?" asked Ali

They all suggested to keep doing what they had been doing: setting traps for the Union's soldiers and killing them. Ali smiled and proposed, "Why don't we find something to eat first? Then we can discuss a plan."

Nora volunteered to bring dinner, going into the woods and tracking the steps of her prey. She recognized the footprint of rabbits and decided to climb a tree to extend her vision. She shot four arrows and didn't miss once, bringing her friends one rabbit for each, which they put on fire.

Alighieri finished first and grabbed a jar of water to drink, and Keita teased him for finishing first. "You eat like you have two right hands."

Alighieri didn't reply but smiled.

After filling their stomachs, Keita asked Ali why he was not so enthusiastic about another attack. Ali coughed twice, drank from a jar, and started talking.

"How many do you think we'll kill until we're caught? A thousand, two thousand? That's less than the number of children they kill in our kingdoms each year. Plus, how different are we from Ceres if we kept killing soldiers who might be innocent? Remember, all they do is obey their chiefs."

Nora and Alighieri didn't dare to disagree with Ali, but Keita did, "Isn't that a necessary evil? They should be aware they are on the evil side!"

"No, my friend, it's not as obvious as you think. A man like Ceres, with power, can turn evil into good. Very few people can take a step back, think neutrally and distinguish between good and evil," explained Ali and continued, "The killing and oppression is Ceres' strength. If we use this technique, he'll defeat us!"

Keita didn't hesitate to ask, "Why do you think he can defeat us?"

"Because, unlike us, he doesn't care about killing children or elders. Nora surrendered to him for the sake of one child, and I don't blame her. On the contrary, I admired her even more because this is who we are, and the world we want to build must have people with these values.

"We should deploy a plan that fits with our values and the world we want to build. For that, I have gathered almost four thousand men and women. They're all in a safe place with King Eleah," Ali concluded.

Nora stood and asked in a surprised tone, "King Eleah is alive?"

Ali nodded. The rebels spent hours asking Ali how he could have gathered all these men and women in the current circumstances and saved the last living king. The three rebels realized that the man sitting next to them was the hope the seven kingdoms had, and they swore to him they would stick with him and only death could break their oath.

Ali had a friend in the Union, who kept informing him of everything happening. The rebels knew they had to stand down and do nothing until he gave the signal that the chasing had stopped. Then, the rebels would sail to the haunted island. Nora was very excited about the idea, trusting Ali blindly, unlike Alighieri.

"These are just commoners, how can the four of us make them soldiers?" asked Alighieri.

Nora couldn't hold herself, "They're men and women with arms and feet, and we're good fighters. It's so simple!"

"A soldier training isn't just about fighting, it's also discipline, obedience, organization…" countered Alighieri.

Nora wanted to reply but Ali went first, "Alighieri, I can't agree more, but for now, it's the only option we have, unless you have a better plan, I'm all ears."

Alighieri smiled and lowered his head.

As for Keita, he was absent-minded, thinking about the haunted Island and the stories he'd heard about it. Ali held Keita's shoulder and told him that everything he heard was a myth made up by people to prevent others from going. Ali also explained that it was the most beautiful land on earth, but he couldn't help Keita to shake the fear from his mind. Alighieri and Nora didn't help and kept teasing him.

Chapter 8

The rats kept scuttling around. Isaac felt disgusted by these creatures, with dirt all over their tiny bodies and their sharp teeth jutting out of their mouths. He was expecting at any moment that one of them would jump and bite him, but they didn't; instead, they were running so fast across the floor making whistling noises.

This kind of fear used to bother Isaac, making him think that he was a coward, but his mother taught him the opposite. She explained that courage is not about swords and fighting, but rather a strong heart that sticks to its believes. Isaac had just realized he was a brave man, as he chose to die rather than kneeling to the emperor. He had a glimpse of hope that his friend Ali might come to his rescue.

While drowning in his thoughts, footsteps caught his ears as someone approached the cell. He wondered if they were soldiers coming to mess with him. Surprisingly, he heard a female voice, which was very unlikely in this kind of place. He tried to listen to what she was saying but couldn't distinguish a word. He wondered if she was a lady friend of one of the guards, but she wasn't, as a few moments after, he saw a shadow of a tall woman walking towards him with a lamp in her right hand.

Her figure got clearer while she was approaching; the green dress with a suede fabric indicated that she was a highborn girl in her twenties, her hair was curly and brown, her blue eyes were sparkling, and so was the blue diamond in her necklace. The guard opened the cell door for the lady and was commanded to leave her alone with the prisoner. Knowing who she was, the guard couldn't question the order.

"I never expected to see a prisoner with a pretty face like yours," said the highborn girl.

Isaac was used to this kind of mockery; with his beardless face and soft golden hair, people didn't miss the opportunity to address insults about his manhood.

He didn't care and chose to respond with a threatening tone, "Appearances can fool people. Remember, I'm a dead man – I would take pleasure in hurting a highborn girl."

"You will never do that," said the girl, "Not because you're weak or a coward – I can tell you're not – but I know you're a decent man, and you would never do such a thing to a girl."

Isaac thought that she threw compliments at him to get something. He made it clear he preferred to die than serve the emperor and described him as a tyrant.

"This is my father you're talking about," reminded the girl.

"You think I care? He's a murderer. You'll go to hell, you and him!" yelled Isaac.

The guards both came running, and one of them asked if she wanted them to beat him.

"If you come again here, I will cut your ears and feed them to the dogs," yelled the princess at the guards. Then she turned to Isaac with a lower tone, "My father doesn't know I'm here. He could use your help, but he's just too proud to ask, so I decided to come here and clear the air between us. We have nothing against you, but this is political: a world with a winner and a loser."

"And what shall I win? Glory, gold?" Asked Isaac.

"Life! Don't you care about it, especially if it is in a castle with women, food, and everything you desire? Spare your life and be part of the biggest empire on earth. Along with us, we'll build a better world".

Isaac wasn't tempted at all and wondered if the lady was just a victim of her father's system, "You know, all these things you said are instinctive desires. Following them will make us no different from beasts, so I choose to believe in justice and a rewarding second life from the creator."

Although Ceres had raised his daughter to believe in the existence of the Gods, she had always been skeptical. "How do you know that there will be a second life?" grimaced the princess.

"And why not?"

The princess felt that Isaac wouldn't change his opinion and decided to cut to the chase, "I never get involved in politics, but since I was assigned to execute you, I came here to offer you a way out. The last thing I like or enjoy is killing people"

Isaac smiled, "Your father had my parents both murdered. If he doesn't kill me, I will kill him."

The princess knew he would never change his mind, "Do you have any death wish?"

Although Isaac knew he was going to die, hearing it from his executioner scared him, he forced a smile, but tears dropped from his eyes.

"What are you afraid of?" asked the princess

"Not death. After all, it's the only certain thing our future holds. But every time I think of the pain that would precede my death, I feel afraid."

The princess' heart softened, but she chose to hide it, "I will make sure to reduce the pain as much as I can."

The princess took her leave, and Isaac was delighted to see that a good, fair heart was close to the emperor.

***

Ramessess was very delighted to have the honor of meeting the emperor in private: it was something rare, and the prime advisor considered it a golden opportunity to learn politics and enhance his long-term vision. But Ceres surprised him when he asked a question Ramessess had never thought about, "Why don't we wipe out the seven kingdoms?"

Empire of Rebels: Rise of Rebels

Ramessess couldn't disappoint his emperor and replied, "Because we need them, your highness!"

Ceres smiled and said, "There's a reason why you're the prime advisor, and you're right. I can't stand seeing other races except our five families on this earth. But we need them. Otherwise, who will clean our stables, build our castles, and heal us from sickness? We're meant to be served by these people!"

Ceres had never underestimated his enemy. No general or king in the seven kingdoms could question his authority or commands. The commoners were under control, or so Ceres thought, as he'd been spreading fear all over the world for a decade. Yet, six rebels appeared out of nowhere and killed more than five hundred soldiers of his.

For Ceres, it was the beginning of the end and he couldn't let it happen, because if he did, things would escalate. People would see his vulnerability and dare to dream of reversing the balance, especially if there was a chief to lead them, and he felt like this leader existed somewhere.

He couldn't share his concerns with Ramessess ; instead, he chose to elaborate on how to stop the rebels before a revolt started, and they came up with an epic plan.

By the time they drank to it, a knock on the gate interrupted. It was a guard with a pale face who was trembling with a box in his hands. Ramessess commanded him to talk, but he couldn't; instead, he kept walking toward the emperor without making eye contact and stopped. When Ceres raised his hand, the guard knelt and opened the box.

The emperor's eyes frowned, he put his hand inside the box and fetched a head that belonged to a commander he recognized.

Ceres chose this commander himself to help Ila arrest the rebels. The head wasn't the only thing in the box: there was a letter, he fetched the parchment and started reading. *"To the beast Ceres. This is just the beginning; I'm coming for you and your dogs. – Ali, or Ila"*

A scream from Ceres filled the council's room. The guard was so scared, thinking his days were over, but he was lucky because Ceres didn't release his anger on him. He instead ordered him to bring the military chief at once. Ramessess couldn't say a word, and at some point, he thought he might not leave the council alive. Luckily for him, Peter didn't delay, he advanced toward the emperor and knelt before him.

He never stood up again. The next thing he felt was the edge of Ceres's blade cutting his neck from behind. When he thrashed like a sheep being slaughtered, Ceres cut the front of his neck and didn't stop until the chief military's head was released from his body.

Ramessess and the guard were in shock, and it wasn't over. Ceres held Peter's hair, made eye contact with him, and said, "That's for making the same mistake twice."

He turned to the guard and told him, "Get rid of this rat immediately."

Ramessess was so scared and eager to leave the council, but he pulled himself together and said, "Your highness, this is a tragedy for our empire. Perhaps you should relax and do some thinking."

The emperor looked at his prime advisor for a while and replied, "No, Lord Ramessess . Nobody will rest until I catch this traitor and take a thousand lives of each soldier he killed."

Ramessess knew it wasn't the right time to plan, but how could he confront his emperor in this state? He chose to sit back and listen, but wished he didn't, because what the emperor said next, shocked every inch of his body, "Lord Ramessess , you're the most trustable man in this empire to me, so I want you to catch this rat yourself, you take as many soldiers as you can, and you bring him to me alive."

Ramessess realized how insane the idea was and dared to disagree politely. "Your highness, my life, and sword are yours. But as your advisor, I must comment on your command, and pardon me for this rudeness." Ceres didn't reply, and Ramessess continued, "Looking for this traitor isn't a good idea, given what he did already. He's probably waiting for us with a trap. I'd suggest finding out what he's planning because that's more dangerous to our empire."

The emperor stood from his seat and went closer to his advisor. "Can you do that?"

Ramessess was relieved and gave his word to the emperor. He was confident he would be successful because he was raised by a princess, Ceres' aunt. Ramessess had the chance to grow in the royal residence and have a special education and training. When he turned eighteen, he joined the soldiers to get stronger, and with his perseverance and ambition, he had made it to a commander at the age of twenty-six. Four years later, Ceres nominated him as a prime advisor. Although the position was challenging, Ramessess was the only man who spent over two decades doing this job brilliantly. Even the new challenge didn't intimidate him because he knew that for each problem, there was a solution. The only things that was required; thinking, perseverance, and consulting his trusted people. He was good at all those things.

Chapter 9

The four rebels marched for almost a day, and Keita was so scared he wished they would never get to the boat. Fortunately, it wasn't that day, as the sunset caught them before reaching the sea. Therefore, they had to camp in the woods, and as usual, the Token girl volunteered to hunt. This time she brought a deer. Delight showed on the rebels' faces, including Keita, and soon their bellies were filled.

Ali seized the opportunity to explain the mission, "First, we must go to the island and meet King Eleah. I will stay there two nights at most and then leave."

"Why the rush? I want to stay longer," said Nora.

Keita understood what the Token girl was doing, but he chose to ignore her.

"There's a man called Isaac, known as the mastermind," said Ali, and they all nodded as a sign of knowing who this man was. "He will be executed in the Kingdom of Solum next week at the latest. I have a plan to prevent his execution."

The three rebels looked at each other in surprise, and Ali understood why they were concerned. Such a mission wouldn't be easy, not even for an army. He decided to reassure them, explaining, "I have eyes everywhere; there will be a hundred soldiers with him."

"And how can the four of us rescue him knowing he will be surrounded by a hundred soldiers?" asked Alighieri.

"It would just be me," replied Ali.

They all looked at him in shock, and Nora jumped, "You're kidding? Right?"

"Relax, the emperor will be with them. A few miles before Solum, he will take most of his men and leave Isaac with approximately thirty soldiers. I have friends everywhere. It will be easy to take him then."

"What about us?" Keita asked.

"Don't worry, Keita, you have something else to do which is certainly not staying on the island. Unlike Nora and Alighieri, they will stay with the king and train the men and women," replied Ali.

The plan didn't suit Ali's companions but couldn't disagree without an alternative one.

The following day, they hit the road and arrived at the sea. Nora and Alighieri were perplexed by its blueness; the waves moved forward like a galloping horse. Keita, however, was silent and scared to death. His friends kept teasing him but they stopped when they saw his state, he was sweating and trembling.

Ali was sure that Keita's fear would disappear the minute they stepped on the beautiful island, with its giant palms, white sand, and safety.

As Ali journeyed through the lush landscape, a dark and ominous cloud on the horizon caught his eye. Fearing the worst, he strained his eyes to see what lay ahead, but the thick smoke obscured his vision. With a sense of urgency, he cried out to his companion, Alighieri, urging him to hasten their journey.

Without hesitation, the Solumy farmer picked up the pace, paddling with all his might. As they drew closer, the true horror of the scene became clear. The once-beautiful palm groves were now ablaze, the fire illuminating the smoke-filled air and casting a dark, eerie glow over the sand.

Without a second thought, Ali pushed Alighieri aside, took control of the boat, and leaped out into the water, running towards the inferno with all his might. His friends followed close behind, but as they approached the first palm, Ali came to a sudden stop, falling to his knees and wailing in despair. Alighieri, horrified, could see what had brought his friend to such a state. Amidst the carnage, a woman's head lay, her brown skin and short hair caked in blood. But it was the tattoo on her forehead that sent a chill down his spine. "Welcome to hell, Ila or Ali," it read. Ali drowned in his sorrows, the regrets eating him from the inside, thinking he was responsible for the death of this woman who had trusted him blindly. He felt a hand tapping his shoulder. When he turned, Alighieri asked softly, "What is it, Ali? Whose head is it?"

Ali turned to him and then extended his sight to Nora and Keita. They were looking at him with worried faces, he wiped his tears, and said "Her name was Andrea, a wonderful and brave woman. She was the chief of the island before King Eleah arrived." Ali ignored their compassion and ran into the forest. They followed him, hundreds of bodies on their way. It smelled of rotting meat, which indicated the attack was a few days ago. They checked every cadaver to see if they could save any, but none were alive. After a few miles, they finally arrived at the village, and to their shock, there was a giant tent in the center. But it wasn't made of fabric. Instead, human bodies burned to the bones. Ali was in shock, running and looking for anyone alive, but with no success. There was one tent that wasn't burned or torn; in no time, they went in, there were two heads hanging on spears.

Ali recognized both and said calmly, "The work of ten years has been destroyed. These are King Eleah and the mastermind, Isaac."

Nora screamed, "Ali, there's a letter in there."

Ali didn't respond, so Keita fetched it and gave it to him.

"To Ali, the rebel.

I have to admit; you have got my attention. But it is this attention that all the seven kingdoms will soon blame you for.

Keep running and hiding like a coward. You will come to me yourself, and it will be the worst death you could ever imagine.

The emperor Ceres"

"What is it?" asked Nora.

"The work of ten years fell out; the secret location was exposed. Our people were burned alive, and King Eleah was executed along with our hope Isaac," replied Ali.

Nora lowered her head and decided not to speak. Neither did Alighieri. However, Keita forgot about the demons on the island and said, "Ali, we can bring more people to another secret place, look for another king. As for Isaac, there are plenty of craftsmen who can do his work."

"Plenty of craftsmen who can do his work!" echoed Ali and continued with a higher tone, "Do you have any idea what this man was capable of? The skills he possessed were worth a whole kingdom."

"What, shitting gold?" asked Keita sarcastically.

"It's a pity you're alive instead of him," replied Ali, and left. He went next to a palm that wasn't touched by the fire and sat there. His companions couldn't leave him in that state and went closer.

They hesitated to speak to him, but Keita dared to go next to Ali to apologize. To his surprise, the Turban stood and hugged him, then said, "If someone has to apologize, it should be me. I'm very sorry for screaming and behaving like a child." The three of them smiled, which encouraged him to continue in a very calm tone, "Isaac had a mind different from any man I've ever met. He held in his hand what was beyond magic. With a small army, we would have reversed the balance and taken down the empire"

Alighieri couldn't hold himself and replied, "How is that possible?"

"He was going to help us build walls that no catapults could take down; make an arrow that can kill ten people at once."

Ali didn't stop there. He kept telling them about Isaac's inventions, which left them agape. Alighieri stood and said, "Ali, what is done is done. Let's think about another plan, but before that, I suggest giving a proper burial to everyone. As for Isaac, let's honor him with a eulogy. I would be delighted to perform the ceremony myself."

They spent three days burying everyone, and when they were done, Alighieri asked them to stand next to Isaac's grave. Each one held the other's hand, and the Solumy farmer started first. "I have never met this man in person, but his reputation reached every land. He's a winner because he chose to stand against evil and gave his life for that."

Nora followed, "What determines a good man isn't his strength or his mind, but rather his heart and Isaac had a brave one. May he be offered a second life!"

Keita shed some tears before speaking, "A wise man once told me our last act is what determines what kind of people we are. I envy Isaac for having the courage to die for what it's right – it is the kind of way I wish to go."

Keita's words moved Ali, and he decided to conclude with a motivating speech, "Maybe we have lost hope to take down the empire, but not a revenge for Isaac and all those who were taken from us." He then raised his tone, "Who wants to go to the forest and track them like beasts?"-

Nora and Keita both screamed "Yes!", but Alighieri didn't; he waited until Ali was done and proposed they take a step back and think about their next move. But they all ignored his advice and chose to move immediately to the forbidden forest and hit back at the emperor.

***

Ceres asked Ramessess how exactly he had accomplished the massacre, and Ramessess proudly stated that he didn't start by gathering an army or hiring mercenaries to respond to the rebels, he instead promised a reward to the citizen who can give helpful information about the gladiator Ila. The next day at noon, there were more than two hundred. Ramessess interviewed each one individually. There were many impostors. He revealed them quickly and chose not to punish them.

Strangely, four of them talked about a carpenter who used to be visited by Ila. Ramessess interrogated him, and the carpenter ended up telling them about the boat he made for Ila and its location. Ramessess could guess that the only destination from the boat's place was the haunted island and was able to decipher Ali's game.

The prime advisor didn't stop there. Instead, he set a plan to attack the island and suggested executing Isaac immediately, and Ceres approved.

Before his death, Issac had been sitting in his cell and had hoped to be rescued by Ali. Although it was nearly impossible, he had faith in his Turban friend.

Two soldiers came to him smiling, and one said, "It's your lucky day; you'll finally get rid of your stupid head."

Isaac didn't reply, the soldiers tied him and pulled him from his arms. He'd never been that afraid in his entire life when he saw the execution yard, which was circular, surrounded by spears engraved in the soil. At the center, there was a tree trunk painted in red, they pulled him and tied him against it.

They used a cord to tie his forehead to it, so his neck could be exposed to the sword.

Ramessess started speaking, "People of the Union, this man has been found guilty of treason. He was working with Ila the rebel; the man who betrayed the empire and was responsible for the death of more than five hundred soldiers.

"Today, this prisoner pays the price for that. He'll be tortured so that he feels the pain of every life he has taken and then executed..."

The prime advisor couldn't complete the sentence – he was cut off by Isaac's screaming, "As long as Ali is alive, you'll never have peace!"

Ramessess was disturbed by the words of Isaac and decided to call the executioner, "Initially, his highness was to execute the traitor himself, but since Princess Leah turned twenty, he wanted her to execute this traitor. She will be using his sword – the Majesty."

Empire of Rebels: Rise of Rebels

She showed up in a white dress with a red flower in the center and the Majesty in her right hand. She approached slowly, standing ten feet away from Isaac.

Ramessess spoke sarcastically, "I thought the creator would come to save you, Isaac."

Isaac hid his fears with a fake smile and replied, "The creator made us all mortal. This is my time, and yours will come one day or another."

Princess Leah stared down at him. "Sir Isaac, do you have a death wish?"

"Princess Leah, he doesn't deserve a title and you should torture him first. Those are his highness' commands," Said Remessess.

Leah ignored the prime advisor and echoed the question.

"Yes, my lady. I want to use my last words as an advice for you and these people," replied Isaac.

Leah nodded.

Isaac started, "I say I'm innocent, and the emperor says I am not. Of course, you agree with your leader, but have you wondered why people like me chose death over a wealthy life in a castle? I am not stupid. Maybe you should consider reading some history instead of listening to your generals and corrupted Speakers...."

"Shoot him!" interrupted Ramessess with a scream.

"Whoever shoots, I'll cut off both his hands," growled Leah, turning to Ramessess, "Lord Ramessess, it's his death wish. Let him speak!"

Isaac continued, "Think about it. Why did Lord Ramessess want to shoot me? Because the truth is a threat to him," he paused, "My lady, I can tell you're a decent person, but you still choose to see the world with your father's eyes?"

Leah said, "tell me, Isaac, have you ever taken a moment to think about what's happening in this world? Every thief, liar, or outlaw comes from the seven kingdoms, while our empire is the place of science; the land that hosts the Speakers." She didn't stop and raised her tone even higher, "This is what my father is trying to build, and what do you do? You sneak to our castle and kill the soldiers who protect you."

"My lady, we might be thieves, liars, outlaws... but go and read our history. Our ancestors weren't like us. They established everything beautiful you see in this world! Yet somehow, we changed and became the outlaws we are now? It was since your father built this empire. Isn't it obvious?"

"So you're the victim here?" Asked Leah.

"Maybe you should ask your father," Issac replied and concluded, "I'm ready to die, my lady."

Leah froze and couldn't move. Isaac decided to help her. "My lady, torturing a man isn't a human, in my heart. I know you're one of the rare decent people in this empire. Kill me instead of playing with my body!"

Ramessess jumped in, "Princess Leah, your father ordered us to torture him for every life we lost because of the rebels."

Empire of Rebels: Rise of Rebels

Leah's hands trembled as she stood before Isaac, the condemned man she had been tasked with executing. Though she knew he was guilty of no crime, the thought of taking another's life filled her with a deep sense of dread. She leaned in close to him, her voice barely above a whisper. "I cannot fathom what death feels like, Isaac, but I swear to make it as quick as possible."

Isaac looked up at her with a serene smile. "I am ready," he said.

With a deep breath, Leah steeled herself, and with all her might, swung her sword at Isaac's neck. His head fell to the ground with a thud and her sword remained embedded in the tree trunk. Blood, bright red and sticky, covered her white dress.

After the execution, Leah retreated to her chambers and spoke to no one. Meanwhile, Ramessess, fueled by a thirst for revenge, gathered an army, set sail with over a hundred ships, and razed the island, slaughtering every living man, woman and child, including the king, Eleah.

CHAPTER 10

Everything was finished for Ali, and he was keen to leave the world of the living, but before that, he would use every skill he'd acquired in his entire thirty-two years to kill as many as he could from the empire. Nora and Keita were excited to join his plan. Alighieri, however, was hesitant – but he was a man of his word, so he preferred to die than break his oath to Ali.

They took their way back to the forest with no precaution; they were like wolves who hadn't eaten for days, all they cared about was the blood of the empire's soldiers. They camped in a cave not so far from a barrack and sat around the fire eating their dinner when Ali decided to speak about the plan of the attack.

He started by telling them a story about a fierce knight called Zeer, who no man could stand against him in a battle. One day his tribe went to war with another tribe who were aware of Zeer's skills and knew that if they wanted to win the war, Zeer must die.

They tried with their best knights, but they never succeeded, they became so obsessed with him that they thought his strength came from his horse or sword. They stole them both, but still, they couldn't even wound him.

When they were about to give up, an old man from another tribe, who was also a great knight, asserted that no man could beat Zeer. They were very upset and considered that the old man was mocking them, but his explanation shut their mouth.

The old knight explained that Zeer's strength came from his carelessness. Once he went in dual, he didn't watch his back; he chose to be entirely focused on his adversary. That dedication was what made him the best fighter of his time.

Ali's companions were focused on the story, and Ali could tell they liked it, "My friends, the story might be entertaining, but that's not why I told it to you. It's rather to show you that fear is an enemy worse than the empire. Ceres had hit us badly, and we need to hit back as well, to regain our confidence.

"As far as I'm concerned, I will fight with all of my power without watching my back, killing as many as I can. In the meantime, I'm freeing you from the allegiance you swore to me."

They all smiled at him and expressed their desire to carry their oath. Ali thanked them and addressed Alighieri, "You're not coming with us."

The Solumy objected, but Ali insisted, "I know how brave you are, but I also know that you disapprove of what we're planning. Go and fight the empire in the way you think is right."

Although Ali's assumption was correct, Alighieri felt he had let his friends down. He tried harder to change the Turban's mind, but couldn't, so he left the three of them and took his way off the following day.

Ali and his companions went to one of the barracks in the west, deciding not to set any traps. Ali assumed the emperor was enjoying the victory, so his tactic was to surround a barrack, fire fiery arrows to distract the soldiers, and attack.

They couldn't be more delighted to see that their first mission was a piece of cake; no soldiers were stationed outside the barrack. They stopped a few hundred feet outside the perimeter, started dipping their arrows into the fire, and aimed for the hut. After the second batch, the fire was already set, but strangely no soldier came out, and Nora whispered, "No one is inside."

"It's a trap. Run!" shouted Ali.

Before they could flee, Ali heard noises in the surrounding trees, and when he looked up, there were two soldiers in each tree with their arrows placed in the bows and ready to shoot. The three rebels fetched their swords and took a fighting position.

Even if they had wings, they couldn't survive. Other soldiers started showing up from trees, at least twenty.

The soldiers stopped, and a man who Ali recognized showed up. It was Ramessess, the most dangerous man after Ceres. He raised his hand to his soldiers and ordered, "No one shoot," then addressed Ali, "Drop your weapons."

Ali thought of disobeying, but he knew he could hardly touch one or two soldiers before the arrows reached him, so he dropped his weapon and so did Keita and Nora.

The soldiers tied them and put them in a cage attached to a wagon. Ramessess spoke with one of his men. "I'm taking off. Don't get closer to them or even talk to them. If they want to piss or shit, they will have to do it in their clothes, understood?"

Ali was very embarrassed and couldn't make eye contact with his friends, but Keita didn't lose hope and started looking inside the cage for a nail or something similar. Nora knew what he was looking for and said, "You can't be that lucky twice! And Sai isn't with us."-

Ali shook his head at Keita. "I placed that nail myself last time, and don't count on Ramessess to do that for us."

Keita stopped and started screaming. His two companions were so embarrassed that they couldn't talk to him, so silence dominated the whole area for a few hours.

After a while, they heard some noises, they couldn't tell what it was, but from the way the soldiers spoke, they seemed angry.

Nora smiled and said, "Maybe it's Alighieri, he's here to save us."

Her assumption was partially correct, as it was Alighieri who was caught by the Union's soldiers. He was pulled from his arms with some bruises on his face. The smile on Nora's face disappeared and was replaced by a look of disappointment when the soldiers got closer, eight of them surrounded the cage and their leader spoke, "Two of my soldiers will open the cage and tie this rat next to you. If anyone tries to be stupid, we'll burn you alive, understood?"

No one answered, but Ali read Nora's eyes and sputtered before they arrived at the cage. "Nora, if you try anything, they'll kill us, so whatever you have in mind, don't do it!."

"We're dying anyway, what difference does it make?" whispered Nora with an angry tone.

"We're keeping ourselves alive, and we'll take a risk if we see a shot. But not now." Ali said, and Nora didn't argue.

Alighieri was tied next to them, and when the soldiers went out, Ali asked, "Why did you follow us?"

"I prefer to die next to my friends," replied Alighieri

Ali smiled back at Alighieri, but that was just on the outside. From the inside, remorse was eating him. He couldn't stand the thought of seeing the emperor relishing victory. In a way, he was eager to have his execution and see what was beyond life, but had to wait another day because the night fell. The soldiers camped in the forest, and the rebels weren't provided any food, but they forgot about the hunger.

Sadness was written all over their faces, so Nora decided to try and lighten the atmosphere, "You know, maybe this is our last night together. What if we say something that could cheer us up?"

Keita was about to speak, and the Token girl interrupted him, "No jokes, Keita!"

"Do you want to comb our hair or play with dolls?" replied Keita.

Alighieri smiled and said, "Keita, she said no jokes. Plus, you're bald."

Nora smiled and said, "Keita, I didn't mean to be rude. Jokes can make us laugh, but there's another thing that can make us leave this cruel world and travel to the perfect place, where all of our senses are shut down except for feelings." She paused and asked, "How come you're all in your twenties or thirties and not married yet?"

Ali had never been asked this question his entire life. "I wish I could, but how can a man love in this world? If I manage to find a girl, we might lead our children to slavery."

Keita was serious for the first time, "No woman would ever accept to marry a Grondy man."

Alighieri interrupted and said, "You could marry a woman from Kingdom of Grond."

"I prefer a Solumy woman," replied Keita, and a peal of laughter filled the cage,

"I tried once. I fell in love with a girl, and I thought she felt the same thing until a wealthy man proposed to her. She accepted, leaving me with a broken heart, so I decided to never try to love again." Said Alighieri

Nora looked at them with a smile and explained, "Love isn't something we control; somehow, it chooses us. When our eyes lay on our soul mates, we can no longer help it. We see the world differently and suddenly possess the secrets to happiness. Of course, it doesn't blind us. We keep seeing the world's cruelty, but it comes accompanied by hope."

"Keita, a decent woman will love you for who you are and what you will be. A princess would kill for a man like you. As for you, Alighieri, she didn't love you. Otherwise, why accept another one?"

Ali finally smiled and asked, "What about you, Nora?"

"He hasn't come yet, but I'm sure he will. If not in this life, maybe the second one."

After a long discussion, they all fell asleep and didn't wake up until the sunshine touched their closed eyes. When they got up, Nora spoke to one of the soldiers to bring them water. He, instead, took off his pants and started peeing next to them. Alighieri held the cage's bars, wishing he could break them and punish the man for taking his pants off in front of Nora.

He didn't have to bother, because when the disgusting soldier was pulling his pants up, an edge of an arrow covered with blood came out of his neck.

Another soldier started screaming, "It's an ambush!"

Ali tried to extend his sight to see where it was coming from and spotted a man standing a few hundred feet away. He couldn't tell who it was, and by the time the soldiers arrived, the shadow had taken his ax and started killing them one by one. Ali knew only one man who could use an ax like that: Arsalan.

Ali was worried about him as he had to face more than ten soldiers, but the Topraki wasn't alone. Two other knights were helping him. One was carrying a spear and piercing every soldier he met, and the other was a hidden shooter. Arsalan and his companions were able to kill all the soldiers.

Nora smiled. "It looks like we're still stuck with each other, but who are they?"

Ali smiled and addressed his companions in the cage, "Aside from you folks, the only three people I know with such courage and audacity are Arsalan, Roulan, and Sai."

Chapter 11

In the morning, the sunlight was warm but not harsh. The birds kept chirping and the breeze was cool as if the universe was replicating Ceres' state of mind. Thinking that the rebels' matter was over.

The emperor gathered his people in the castle's bailey.

Thousands of the Unionists formed ranks like an army in a battle. They were not carrying swords but flowers in all forms and colors. Delight filled the yard, and Ceres showed up on the balcony with a crown on his head and an orange robe. His three daughters were on the left, and his wife and the heir were on the right. Screaming filled the place and the people cheered him up even more. The smile did not disappear from his face; he waited a moment, then raised his hand to speak,

"People of the Union, today is another glorious day that will mark history. The five gods chose to be on our side once again. Why? Because we are trying to build a better world, despite all the challenges we're facing.

Our enemy does not like seeing the earth in its great shape. All they care about is destruction, but it is over. Or is it?"

Ceres paused and continued, "Maybe we won this battle against the rebels, but do you know how many widows are in our empire now? How many children won't have the chance to see their fathers again? These rebels brutally killed hundreds of our loyal soldiers, and they are still free."

The crowd screamed with three words to find, catch, and kill them.

"And then what?" asked the emperor, "Other rebels will attack again, and we won't realize it until they take another thousand soldiers. We'll keep going in a circle. But I'm not accepting that anymore.

"When a body is injured, healers don't deal with just the blood. Rather, they tried to find a way to close the wound, and that's what I decided to do after seeking the counsel of my advisors.

"We will fight these rebels from the source; in their kingdoms.

"I was merciful with the seven kingdoms and understanding of their traditions. I let them rule in their own way, but now there is a lack of management.

"I, Emperor Ceres of the house of Wud, decided to nominate Lord Ramessess from the house of Sua for this mission. He will start with the Kingdom of Dharatee and Turang. Please join me to congratulate the new king."

Ramessess showed up wearing a robe with the official colors of Dharatee, white and blue. He knelt before

Ceres, who placed a crown on his head. Everyone was enjoying the joyful atmosphere except Princess Leah.

She was next to her two younger sisters. Her face was pale, and she kept pretending to smile during the whole ceremony until she got in her room. While she was trying to remove her dress, a servant came in and said, "Princess Leah, your father wants to speak with you!"

Leah asked her to close her dress zipper and went straight to the council. The guard let her in. She walked towards her father and asked, "You wanted to see me, your highness?"

"Whenever you call me by your highness, I know something is wrong."

"Forgive me, father, it was a tiring day!" replied Leah.

"Something else is bothering you, and I bet it has to do with the execution of Isaac."

Ceres' eyes pushed into her, and Leah couldn't hold it in anymore, "Why this obsession of controlling the whole world, father? You have the biggest castle and army, dominating the economy and every industry, and now you want to colonize them?"

If it were for anyone else, Ceres would have cut his head off, but it was Leah. She was the puppet of his eyes, so he decided to tell her what he told his people. "Sweetheart, they are unable to control their rebels, so I must intervene. Otherwise, we would undergo tougher consequences."

"Have you ever wondered why they're attacking us?"

Ceres kept calm and answered with a question, "And have you ever asked yourself why only seven of them are trying to attack us?" Then continued, "No, you have not. So let me explain it to you. These outlaws are thirsty to kill. Plus, why attack soldiers doing their job if they have a problem with me or my generals? I can assure you that if one of them meets a child, he will not hesitate to take its life."

Leah could not reply, and Ceres held her in both arms and said, "The politics are so complicated, but you have to trust me."

"I'm sorry, father, if I misjudged you. It's because I care about you, and I want to keep seeing you as my hero," replied Leah.

Ceres hugged her, and after a long chat, they had dinner together and went to their chambers.

Leah was relieved and somehow understood that her father was not evil like Isaac tried to explain to her. She realized that Ceres did what he saw best for his people.

On these thoughts, the princess fell asleep and dived into a dream where she met Isaac. He was wearing a robe in green and white color. She turned and realized that she was in the forest. She grabbed a stick and took a position of fighting.

Isaac smiled at her and said, "Relax, Princess Leah, you can't kill me twice!"

"What do you want from me?" asked Leah.

"You should probably ask yourself what I am doing in your head. Remember, you already killed me," replied Isaac, then asked, "Maybe you're feeling guilty?"

"Why should I? You were an outlaw. I killed you to save other lives from your attacks," Replied Leah.

"Why was there no trial for me?" asked Isaac. Leah could not answer. "Your father keeps telling you lies. Don't let your love for him blind you. He is selfish and evil, and if you disagree, ask him yourself why he butchered one of his most trustable advisors, Peter."

"He didn't do his job properly," said Leah.

"And why are you ashamed of seeing his daughter Sofia, who is your only friend in this world?" asked Isaac

"Do you want me to kill my father?"

"Do you want to do that?" asked Isaac back.

"I only want to understand!"

"Start by doubting everything around you, and don't ask the rebels or your father," said Isaac and disappeared.

Leah started screaming, "Wait, wait…" she didn't stop until she felt a hand on her shoulder. Leah opened her eyes to the face of her servant.

"It's alright, my lady. It was just a dream", said the servant.

Leah drank water and started processing the dream, which disturbed her. She felt like her father and Isaac were taking her in two opposite directions.

Leah had always doubted the things around her. She grew up without a mother, who had passed away when she gave birth to her. The princess had no memory of her, and she regretted that because she knew that a mother was the only one who could answer a daughter's questions in the dark and confusing moments.

Her loneliness was interrupted by the gardener, who was watering the plants and cutting the grasses. She opened the window and spoke loudly, "Good morning, Uncle Rio."

"Good morning, princess! Am I interrupting your peace and quiet?" replied Rio.

Leah smiled at him, "On the contrary. Without you, the greenery in this garden wouldn't last a week!"

Rio smiled and lowered his head.

"May I join you, Uncle Rio?"

Rio raised his head and smiled, "I'd be honored, my princess"

Leah went down in no time and Rio stopped working when he saw her and smiled, "It seems like the princess has a question?"

Leah nodded and asked, "How do you know if you're a good or bad person?"

"It's something you already know, but the confusion comes when you expose your mind to the thoughts of others," replied Rio, but Leah didn't understand, so he picked a red flower and handed it to her. She took it to her nose and enjoyed smelling it with closed eyes.

"What do you think of this flower? Is it dead or alive?" Asked Rio.

"It smells incredible and looks more beautiful than this castle, so it's alive," replied Leah.

"Then what would you say about a man who got the ugly sickness? Dead or alive?"

Leah thought for a while and replied, "Healers say that this disease takes a man's life in less than a month, so he's a dead man."

Rio smiled, "And that goes for the flowers too. In a few days, it would die, so we can also consider it dead," Leah smiled and invited him to continue, "Both answers are correct. Each corresponds to a specific context that only you can determine, but if you let someone else answer instead of you, that's when the confusion starts."

Leah loved the explanation the gardener gave to her. She realized that her father and Isaac had been pulling her in opposite directions; if she didn't decide which direction she needed to take, she would end up torn apart.

Leah decided to change the subject to something that had been obsessing her since she had met Isaac. "Tell me, Uncle Rio, how did the world start?"

Rio put down the watering can and looked at her strangely, then replied with a lower tone, "My princess, this is not something a gardener can answer. It's a very complex matter, even for a Speaker."

"I know how wise you are. You're only avoiding giving an answer because my father has prohibited talking about such matters. I promise you whatever you say ,it will remain between us."-

"My princess, my parents told me that thousands of years ago, a man and woman were living in the skies, and an invisible power brought them down to earth to inhabit it. They were our great-grandfather and grandmother," replied Rio.

"So you believe in the creator, Uncle Rio?"

The gardener nodded. He begged her not to tell anyone, she promised him she would not and asked him to elaborate on his response.

"There must be a creator, my princess. I mean, we humans could not come from nothing?"

"Then who created the creator?" asked Leah.

Rio liked this question and forgot himself, so he dared to ask the emperor's daughter, "What if you tell me what you think, princess?"

"I think there's no Creator. We just came to this universe and evolved with it."

"So, you believe in the existence of something that has no beginning?" asked Rio

"Yes, the universe – it has always existed!"

Rio smiled, "We are on the same page, my princess. The difference is how we describe the origin of everything. You choose randomness, and I prefer an intelligent power: the creator."

Rio realized that he had gone too far. If somehow the princess got upset, he might lose his life, so he apologized.

She smiled at him and said, "Relax, Uncle Rio. If only all men who believe in the creator were like you, I wouldn't have any problem believing in him. Even if he is just a fraud, I will lose nothing . But my mother died because of him. His servant tricked my father and took my mother's life because I was born, they told him, a life must be taken if he wanted an heir."

Rio sighed, "There you go again, submitting your mind to others! You were not there."

Leah smiled, and Rio wanted to cheer her up, "I remember your mother, a good woman. She was sweet and humble like you!"

They carried the discussion for some time, then Leah handed him the red flower and excused herself, returning to her chamber. After the instructive exchange she had with the gardener, she cleared her mind of every doubt and decided to follow her father's quest. She saw the success he brought to the empire and how he cared about every individual in it. Besides that, he was a human who has the right to make mistakes.

In the afternoon, she wore her golden knight suit and went to her father. She was let in by the guards to the council. All the generals stood, and Leah went closer to her father, knelt, and said, "If the offer is still standing, I'd like to join the council."

Ceres stood and took her hand, then he redirected his sight to a chair on his right, "Darling, this chair has always been empty, because it has always been yours!"

Chapter 12

Arsalan had the chance to grow up in a noble family in the Kingdom of Toprak. At twenty-two, he was appointed as a leader, the sixth rank in the Topraki army, and took his job with passion until the poison of the empire started spreading to his kingdom.

The emperor wiped out their identity and traditions; no one in Toprak could do anything without the empire's blessing.

Arsalan had had enough when he learned that his promotion ceremony to commander had to be done in the Union. He decided to leave the Kingdom of Toprak with his wife and son for a piece of land owned by his family, where he found the pleasure of farming, distancing himself from politics.

Arsalan and his wife couldn't have been happier, spending their days sowing and reaping their land, and raising their child. The Topraki realized how life was simple away from politics, because the minute he stepped aside, everything went in the right direction. He could see a bright future with many sons and daughters.

On the flip side, they suffered homesickness; at every feast, sadness filled their hearts thinking about the beautiful memories of their old life. It remained so until the Spring feast when Arsalan decided to surprise his wife.

He woke up early in the morning and went to the closest market: to buy food, supplies and collect some flowers. Then went to a cabin in the woods, which he built a week before, he surrounded it with flowers and hung many candles inside. He was eager to see the look on his wife's face when she would see all the preparations he did for her.

On Arsalan's way back, he saw many Union's soldiers at the entrance of his farm. His heart started pumping as he galloped towards them with his ax in his right, willing to cut everyone, and before arriving, a soldier raised his hand and spoke, "Get off your horse and hand over your weapon."

Arsalan got off his horse, but he didn't give up his ax. Instead, he advanced with an angry look, and the soldier spoke again, "If you make another step, she will die."

Another soldier was pulling his wife from her hair, while she was screaming, "They killed our boy! Save yourself and avenge us later!"

Arsalan could hardly stand on his feet, but he didn't drop a tear and maintained his ax in his hand.

"I said drop your weapon, or I will slaughter her," commanded the soldier.

His wife echoed her message, making Arsalan confused. In his mind , he knew his wife had a point if he surrendered, they would both die. If not, she would surely die, but he might have a chance to avenge her and his boy.

His heart outweighed his mind, and he couldn't leave his wife, obeying the Union's soldiers.

The minute they took his ax and tied him, another soldier brought his wife a few feet away from him, she was screaming, "Don't give up my love!"

Arsalan pleaded, "Please let her live, and you can deal with me"

"You should have thought about this when you left your duty," replied the soldier while cutting her throat.

Arsalan's screaming was like a lion's roar when it's hungry. He didn't stop until he fainted, then woke up in a cell. He was eager to quit the world of the living.

While Arsalan was in the dungeon expecting his execution the following day, he realized his time hadn't come yet, as the door of his cell had been unlocked. He assumed it was due to the new king's celebration in the city, but then a parchment was thrown to him by a soldier.

"Save yourself to avenge your family and prevent other innocent to die"

Arsalan followed the advice and ran away.

Like Nora, he struggled initially, trying to escape from the bounty hunters. The king put a hundred gold coins as a prize for his head. He'd sought refuge in the forest far away, and it hadn't taken him long to regain his confidence. He dared to enter the forbidden forest, attacking from the south by setting traps and burning barracks.

Arsalan's circumstances made him resent the empire, and he could no longer stand people, even the good ones. Losing his family made him forget how to value decent people. In better circumstances, he would have bent the knee to a great man like Ali, but he chose to leave him and get back to killing the empire's soldiers. Thankfully, by chance, he met with Roulan and Sai who were tracking Ali's capturers. They set a trap for the Union's soldiers and took them down, as a result, Ali and his three companions were rescued.

Arsalan spotted a soldier moving, and he remembered that he had only hit him with his ax's handle. The Topraki went to finish him, and the soldier screamed, "Please don't kill me. I have an old mother to look after."

Arsalan didn't care, but when he was about to cut him, a voice came from behind, "He surrendered. No need to shed more blood!"

Arsalan turned to see whose words they were, they were Ali's.

Ali ran toward the soldier and helped him to stand. He gave him water and asked if he could walk to his family. The Unionist stood and ran a few feet, and when no one followed him, he realized that the rebel was serious, so he stopped and said, "My name is Eliot from the house of Nasr. This is a debt I can never pay, but I will die trying. Farewell, good fellows!"

The four survivors thanked their rescuers. Roulan and Sai were delighted to hear all their compliments, but not Arsalan. He didn't even smile and spoke dryly, "I'm not your friend, and I was here by coincidence. Be careful next time!"

"Why don't you have dinner with us and leave tomorrow? It won't cost you anything," said Nora.

Arsalan looked at her and replied, "Next time, think before you speak!"

Nora approached him a few feet and exploded on his face, "I think before I talk, commander. I'm aware of your losses, and I'm deeply sorry about them! But you're not the only one here who has lost his family. I watched the execution of my father and two brothers, and my mother was hanged in her room, but I chose to move on and try to do what's right."

"And what did you do?" asked Arsalan and carried on sarcastically, "You got caught by the emperor's dogs."

Ali interrupted the debate and asked Arsalan, "Why don't you want to join us?"

"Firstly, I can't make an alliance with people from Turba and Grond. Remember, you were the ones who conspired against our kingdom," replied Arsalan.

Arsalan was expecting Ali to get into the debate, but he didn't. Instead, he asked him something different, "I know you're a decent man and a brave knight. So give me a chance to prove to you that our cause is worth more than a kingdom. It's going to take you two days. Can you do that?"

The Topraki didn't reply. He instead went next to a tree and laid down while the others continued the discussion. In the beginning, it was pleasing, especially with Keita's jokes. But it turned into something scary when Roulan explained that things had been twisted in her kingdom, Turang.

When they were on their way back to Turang, they met some people who informed them about the new decision the empire took towards the two kingdoms; Ramessess was placed as a new king. In other words, Turang and Dharatee officially became parts of the Union.

While everyone was processing what Roulan said, Ali understood the emperor's strategy and shared it, "Don't worry, Roulan. He could never do that, or at least for the time being. His intention was to turn the Dharatian and Turangies against us.

He's afraid that they will consider what we, the rebels, did was heroic; he can't let that happen, because there will be more revolts that threaten his empire. So he decided to make people's lives more miserable and explained his actions as measures of protection against rebels, therefore, the commoners will blame us for that."

Nora stood and asked, "What should we do?"

"Stay alive and persuade Arsalan to join us!" replied Ali.

The following day, they took their way expecting to see the sea because the only potentially safe place could be on an isolated Island, but they were going in the opposite direction. Keita and Nora kept asking where they were going, but Ali had only one answer, "You will find out soon."

The sunset was close, and they all assumed they wouldn't reach their destination that day. Suddenly Ali stopped, and a smile crossed his lip.

"Are you going to kill us?" asked Keita.

"We arrived!" said Ali.

They were all confused because the place was unremarkable. In other words, it was a massive piece of land with a few trees in the center. While they were looking for clues, Ali advanced toward a tree in the center and decided to finally shed some light.

"My friends, this is the Blessing Tree: a gateway to the Thinkers." Ali felt like he was talking in a different language. So he asked them all to sit around the tree and held each other's hands, forming a circle around the Blessing Tree.

Ali instructed them to close their eyes and think about beautiful memories.

Alighieri thought about the girl he loved; Giulia was her name, blond, with golden hair and brown eyes.

Keita chose to think about his kingdom when he was less than ten, the large yard in their house and his mother's beautiful face.

Nora couldn't think of anything as beautiful as her father.

Roulan and Sai's most beautiful memory was how their love story began.

Arsalan could not place anything beautiful in his mind, unlike Ali, who chose to think about beautiful things that had not happened yet. He was thinking of a new kingdom that would reunite the seven ones and take down the empire.

The earth seemed to whirl around them, and the next thing they saw was the inside of a cave. It was a very strange one. For starters, the light was so warped: there was no hole to let the sunshine in, yet it felt like they were sitting on a roof exposed to a sky with no clouds. It smelled like lavender there, but there was no plant inside.

They all started asking what was going on, and Ali was just smiling and didn't say a word. Suddenly, a male deep voice filled the cave, "Welcome to the universe's heart."

Everyone tried to locate the source of the voice, but there was no one else. Alighieri looked at Ali and asked him, but the Turban kept silent, and Nora shouted, "Say something!"

"He can't speak, and neither should you," said the voice

"So show yourself!" yelled Nora, then she felt her lips stuck together.

"You speak only if you're asked to," replied the voice, and Nora's lips were released. No one dared to say another word and silence dominated for a while. Then the voice started talking without revealing whose it was, "Ali brought you here because he has placed his trust and hope in you!" The voice gave permission to the guests to speak.

Alighieri started and asked diplomatically, "We're your guests, we follow your rules. But can we at least know who you are?"

"Didn't Ali tell you who we are?" asked the voice.

Roulan intervened, "All he said was that you are some sort of Thinker, but we've no idea what that is. At least tell us from what kingdom you are."

The voice replied, "My dear Roulan, a kingdom is just a name given to a land by some men once. The Thinker's identity is Good."

Arsalan didn't like what was happening and asked Ali to help them leave.

"Lord Arsalan, come closer and put your right hand on the wall," commanded the voice. Arsalan looked at Ali, who nodded, and the Topraki did as he was asked. By the time he touched the wall, the place around him had changed into a chamber with white walls. He was scared and released his hand, looking at Ali who smiled and said, "You won't regret it, you have my word."

Arsalan put his hand again on the wall and didn't release this time. He saw himself in a big chamber. Its walls and roof were bright white, and he could see nothing else, not even his reflection. His mind could not process what was happening and he could only hear his breath.

After a while, a woman with golden hair and blue eyes showed up. She was wearing a white dress. Arsalan could tell that she was from Kingdom of Solum like Alighieri, so he dared to ask who she was. To his surprise, she claimed to be his great-grandmother.

His mind couldn't process the thought, though his heart believed her somehow. He felt different in that place, there was no anger or rage inside him. So he smiled, and the blond woman smiled back, "Come with me, son!"

Although he'd never seen his mother, the lady's voice reminded him of her. A tear finally dropped out of his eye, and his grandmother wiped it using her right thumb. "She's proud of you. You never left her eye, even in the other world!"

They kept walking toward the wall with no door, but they walked through it to a strange land. There was no greenery. Instead, rocks with a color ranging from gray to dark brown. They kept walking and saw a vast castle that looked like the one he had seen once in the Kingdom of Solum. The lady confirmed that this was the same kingdom. Arsalan looked at her strangely, and she said, "Yes, you were once a Solumy, and three hundred years later, my grandson married a Turban princess. Their grandchildren ruled for centuries the two kingdoms, and it kept going like that until one of your great-grandmothers married a Topraki who was your sixth grandfather."

Arsalan lowered his head, feeling ashamed by learning that his origins were from Solum and his blood contained Turbans – the people he hated most, "So I'm from the Kingdom of Solum?".

"No, you're who you want to be, which is clearly a Topraki," reassured the blond woman.

"But my blood has other kingdoms'?" Asked Arsalan

"Remember, humanity came from one man and one woman. After all, we all have the same blood, but you're a Topraki because you have memories there. Your mother's and father's, the soil you used to play in when you were kid, the feasts you celebrate, the food you love," replied the blond lady, "But being Topraki isn't what makes you bad or good, rather it's your heart; those who were blessed with your kindness and courage are your brothers and sisters. You must die protecting them, wherever they're from"

He kept looking at her and asked, "What should I do?"

"Follow your heart, and don't leave a place for ego, hatred, or sadness. You're meant for a great cause."

The next thing Arsalan saw was the face of Nora, who was trying to wake him up, and to her surprise, he smiled, which was unusual. He looked around and realized they were no longer in the cave, but in the forest.

Alighieri gave him his hand to help him stand, and Arsalan went for a hug. The Solumy understood nothing, but he didn't mind. Then Arsalan went toward Ali and said, "Ali, whose voice was that? And what was that place?"

"He's one of the Thinkers. They were once men, spending their entire lives serving humanity, and when their spirits left their bodies, the creator brought them to the heart of the universe. So they could guide confused people like you."

"But I was a bad man!" asked Arsalan.

"No, you were lost as I was few years ago. Because of your decent heart, a Thinker accepted to host and guide you."

Arsalan advanced towards Ali and knelt, "My ax and my life are for you as long as you follow this cause."

Ali held him by his shoulder and replied, "Never kneel before anyone, my companion."

"What's next, Ali?" Nora asked.

"That would depend on Sai," replied Ali and turned to Sai. "Sai, how far would you go for our cause?"

"If I have a hundred lives, I wouldn't mind giving them all to see a tiny hope of victory against the empire," replied Sai.

Ali stared at Roulan, who understood that Ali was asking for her blessing, and she admired him even more for caring about love in these challenging circumstances, so she replied,

"If he died serving our cause, I would consider this as an honor, and it would be like a crown on my head."

"Sai is extremely talented with plants. If I'm not mistaken, he used to make breathtaking perfumes?" asked Ali.

Roulan retrieved a flask and handed it over to Nora, who smelled it and couldn't open her eyes. "I was raised in a castle, and I've never smelled something as good as this perfume."

Ali decided to cut to the chase, "It's true that Sai is an excellent fighter, but his talent is for crafts and science. I'm not the only one who said that. Even Thinkers felt that. So we thought Sai might take over what Isaac had started."

Sai couldn't believe what he had just heard. He even made Ali swear he wasn't messing with him. Although the Dharatian had always felt very confident with tools, replacing Isaac was very intimidating. "I'm thrilled by this proposal, and there's nothing I want more than doing something like that, but I'm nothing compared to Isaac."

"He was once a powerless baby, and he learned, so could you," replied Ali, "You will be trained by Speakers. They will help you see many secrets in this world, and I'm sure you have what it takes to learn."

Sai couldn't say a word, and Ali suggested that his other companions give the Dharatian some privacy with his wife.

Roulan had mixed emotions, proud of Sai for carrying the responsibility of the whole world on his shoulders, but sad because she won't see him for a while. She pulled herself together and said, "Be a quick learner and come back to me." Tears fell for both of them.

The following day, Ali gathered his companions and spoke, "Sai and myself are going to the Speakers, so I will be absent for weeks. I suggest we place a new leader. Will you accept my choice?"

"You're our leader. Your commands are not discussable," replied Keita.

"I'm not that kind of leader. You can question any decision," replied Ali.

"Then what's the point of having a leader?" asked Arsalan.

"To make sure everyone is on board!" replied Ali and continued, "I suggest Alighieri, not because he's the bravest among you, but rather because he's the wisest. He was the only one to control his anger and rage when we saw the island's attack."

"Maybe he should be our leader even after you're back," joked Keita.

Ali replied in a serious tone. "If that's what you want, I will step out now."

Keita didn't reply, but Alighieri did, "What I care about is our cause, which is freeing people from the emperor's evil. There's no man on earth who can lead such a cause as you, Ali!"

No one could disagree with Alighieri.

CHAPTER 13

Ali and Sai hit the road before the sunset and didn't speak for a while. Before, the Turban had given Sai some space to prepare for the separation with his wife. The sadness was in his eyes, which also hid some delights in his heart.

Sai was thinking about his new mission, and the work of a craftsman which had always been his dream. He remembered the old days with his father who was a multi-skilled man; a healer, perfumer, and a blacksmith.

Sai wanted to learn everything at once, but his father taught him to be organized and learn one thing at a time. Perfumery was the most minor thing Sai wanted to learn, yet his father insisted on starting with it. He wanted him to learn the names of each flower in the seven kingdoms; how to extract its perfume and isolate the poison.

From time to time, Sai sneaked to his father's other shops to learn black-smithing and how to make ointment. His father was aware of it but pretended not to, because somehow he saw that his son had a beautiful mind which could understand how things work without a teacher to guide him.

Sai's life was taking a direction, every child his age would wish for it. Unfortunately, the empire's power had started spreading and left no one to live peacefully.

When Sai's father and the villagers refused to pay taxes, the new king of Dharatee sentenced everyone to death, and Sai was the only one to survive. He was away collecting some plants when the slaughter happened.

The Dharatian rebel was young. He managed to run to the city and hide; he grew up in its streets and used every means necessary to remain alive. As a result, he forgot every value his mother or father taught him, and stealing for living became the only thing he was good at. It didn't bother him, until he met the love of his life Roulan, who opened his eyes to the beauty of the world.

Thanks to her, he was living for the most significant cause on earth, which was fighting evil.

Although Ali had never been in love, he could tell that Sai's eyes were hiding something mysterious. He also was aware that the Dharatian was very excited about his new mission, so Ali decided to intrigue him, "Do you know that if we keep going on a straight line, we'll return to our place in less than a year,"

It did intrigue Sai, and before he asked for further details, Ali interrupted him, "This is a tiny thing compared to what you are going to learn from the Speakers."

After they left the forest, everything they passed through was new to Sai.

Unlike his home and the places he'd been to, which were lands with forests, mountains, and hills. The places they were walking on were strangely different. Sand dunes formed the shape of hills. He had heard many stories about people who went to the desert and never made it back alive.

Sai couldn't help but ask his companion, "How do you know your ways in this land that has nothing except sand?"

"There are different ways, like the position of the sun by day and stars by night, prevailing wind, and so on."

Sai had an ear for the details and noticed that Ali explained how other people did it, not him, so he doubted that his companion had a mysterious tip. Sai was enjoying everything, but not for long, as he was interrupted by an unpleasant statement from Ali, "Now that we're out of the desert, we're no longer safe from the empire's soldiers."

Ali pointed his finger to a mountain not so far away and said they needed to spend the night in one of its caves. The Dharatian was exhausted and not in a state to keep walking, but he felt he had no choice. It was about a mile before they reached their destination, and Ali held his friend's arm and put his index on his lips.

Sai didn't move or talk, instead he took his bow and placed an arrow there. They expected someone to come out at any time. A shadow of a man appeared, unarmed and thin, yet Ali was very cautious. He went slowly with his sword and placed it on the man's neck, "Speak!"

The man couldn't speak, trembling, and tears were coming from his eyes like the drops of heavy rain on a window.

Ali kept waiting to hear words, and when they finally came to his ears, he couldn't distinguish any because of the stranger's whining. The Turban wanted to lower his sword, but he was afraid the man was just pretending. Surprisingly, a voice came from behind, "Advik!"

Ali turned, and to his surprise, Sai seemed to know the man. "Ali, this is a friend of mine. Please lower your sword, he's a good man."

Ali did, and Sai went straight to the crying man and hugged him. He then pulled him from his hand and told Ali, "This is my friend Advik. We used to live together," Sai smiled, although his friend Advik didn't.

"Advik, you're safe. This is my friend Ali," Sai was trying to reassure his friend. Ali looked Advik in the eyes and asked him why he was that far from Dharatee.

Advik finally stopped whining and said, "I ran away to save my boy."

Ali and Sai looked at each and then at Advik, who continued, "The emperor has placed a new king for Dharatee. He goes by the name of Ramessess . It didn't bother us much because even the previous king was the emperor's puppet. But what was horrific was the new law they released; no family in our kingdom can have more than one child!"

Sai went furious. "How is this possible? Everyone who gets married can only hope for one child?"

"That would be a mercy compared to what he did to us," replied Advik, and Ali asked him immediately to elaborate, and he did by saying, "Every family who has more than one child will have to give the additional kid to the army of the Union," He started crying and continued, "And I couldn't let them take my other child, so I ran away with my family."

Hearing this made Ali realize that his cause had been more weakened than ever, but decided not to make the same mistake and react immediately. He instead chose not to do anything until he cleared his mind of anger.

They found a cave and decided to spend the night in it. After eating, Sai and Advik went to sleep, but not Ali. He went out, laid down, and kept looking at the sky. It was very clear, and the view of the stars was taking him away from his sorrow, to thinking about his life which was a total disaster, being enslaved at an early age. He would never forget his first days in slavery: he was barely thirteen years old the first time he had been given a sword to fight a gladiator who had no mercy in his eyes.

Fortunately for Ali, the fighter was instructed not to kill him, but he enjoyed punching Ali, causing some real bruises on his body. Ali disobeyed them and swore that he would never fight.

He was keen to die and join his mother, but the gladiators' leader was familiar with this kind of behavior and knew how to deal with it. The master tried to torture Ali, but the little man resisted all sorts of pains, such as removing his nails. The one he hated most was waterboarding, but his strength drove his leader mad – though he was impressed by the resilience of Ali ,who was thirteen years old. So the leader decided not to give up and use his last card, asking two soldiers to bring him to his chamber.

When Ali arrived, the leader asked the soldiers to unchain him, and invited Ali to sit down in front of him.

"Why don't you want to fight?" asked the leader.

"I know you earn a lot of gold behind these fights, and I would never give that opportunity to you. I'd rather die," hissed Ali.

The leader smiled and asked in a sarcastic tone, "And I assume you're expecting death to be better than life, right?" Ali didn't answer, the leader continued, "I won't argue with you on that, death would be a mercy for you. But I'm not going to kill you."

This time, Ali decided to reply. He said, "What worse can you do to me, pig?"

The leader controlled his anger and replied with a smile, "Here's the thing, my boy, I'm not going to kill or torture you. I'll make you a slave for a highborn woman. Most men would kill for that. I mean living among a hundred young and beautiful girl servants, but not you. because you will no longer be a male."

Ali was terrified and couldn't imagine a single day in that state, and he was easily persuaded to start fighting. His only condition was to have his first training fight with the muscled man, who used to beat him, and his wish was granted.

The following day, Ali showed up in a different state than before. He was wearing red trousers and long black boots, he was shirtless, and his right hand was holding a sword. His opponent laughed at him and said sarcastically, "I'm scared of this boy."

"You should be you're instructed not to kill me, but I'm not."

Ali ran toward his opponent with his sword. The giant man held Ali's right hand, took his sword, and punched him in the face until he fell on his back.

The gladiator was holding Ali's sword and started making fun of him, "And now, how are you going to kill me?"

Ali stood and walked a few steps backward. Those watching assumed that the little fighter was frightened, but he proved them wrong when he sprinted toward his opponent. Before reaching him, he slid and punched him hard between his legs.

The gladiator folded over with pain, and by the time he pulled himself together, Ali had fetched a knife hidden in his back and stabbed him. The giant turned and slapped Ali, who didn't fall this time; rather, he pierced his opponent twice in the chest and waited until he fell on his knees. The little slave didn't let the giant man throw his last breath in peace. Instead, he cut his neck and turned his face to his leader with hands covered in blood.

The leader looked at Ali proudly and knew that this boy was extraordinary. He was right, because within two years, Ali conquered the Arena, and no one could stand against him.

Years went by. Ali loved the blood more and more until the day he witnessed a duel between a tiny man who was taken from the Kingdom of Toprak against a gladiator. The Topraki dropped his weapon and said, "I have two children. If you kill me, they will grow up with no father."

The gladiator didn't care and broke his neck.

This event twisted Ali's mind, making him question everything, starting with the world's injustice. The first time he asked a Speaker why some people were born in castles and spent their entire lives being spoiled at every level, while others were submitted to slavery. The Speaker explained that the world was cruel. They said weak people stood no chance to live in it.

It never made sense to Ali, thinking about his life, which seemed like a tragedy in the beginning, but somehow turned differently. Starting with how he survived the Arena mortal combats, since he was fourteen; not to mention his owner, a woman called Bianca who bought him and was like a mother to him.

When Ali turned twenty, she freed him, but he chose to remain with her. The day Ali witnessed the murder of the Topraki, he went to Bianca and asked her permission to leave the empire free like she promised him.

"I'm a woman of my word," said Bianca and handed him his freedom certificate.

Ali took it and without reading the content, knelt before Bianca, thanking her.

"Where do you want to go?" asked Bianca, while she was trying to hold back her tears.

Seeing Bianca's tears weakened Ali. He came to her, kissing her hand, "I don't mean to leave you my lady, but

I no longer want to kill for fun. There are so many questions in my mind!"

Bianca wiped her tears and replied with a smile, "Don't worry about me, it's just hard for me to no longer see you. It has been eight years, and I've gotten used to seeing you around!"

"I promise to come back the minute I find answers!" replied Ali

To his surprise, Bianca fetched a parchment with a map and showed him the Blessing Tree, where he could find all the answers he was seeking.

Ali left the empire aiming for the Blessing Tree which took him three weeks to find. Ali went to the tree trunk and did what he was told, and upon his waking, he found himself in a very strange cave.

A man was standing in front of him, wearing a white robe, with black, long hair and a thick beard. He was surrounded by a light like a moon.

"Where am I? And who are you?" asked Ali

"You're in the heart of the universe. And I'm a Thinker!" replied the man

"A Thinker?"

"I was once a man. When I died, a power resurrected my spirit along with three hundred and twenty-three men, gathered here to guide the people willing to do good and fight evil!" replied the Thinker.

"Why don't you fight evil yourself?" asked Ali.

"Earth has always been inhabited by humans. Some of them like you are responsible for evil and good,"

Ali looked at the Thinker, surprised, and asked, "It's all too complicated, I want to remain neutral."

"There's no such a thing as neutral. If you don't act against evil, you will be part of it,"

"Why would I care? It's other people who started it," countered Ali.

The Thinker decided to persuade Ali metaphorically, "Who would you praise more? A man who possesses two silver coins, he shares one and keeps the other for himself, or another man who have a thousand gold coins, and shares a hundred?"

"The first one, since he gave half of what he possessed!" replied Ali.

"No man fights as good as you. Your mind is as sharp as Ceres', and your heart refuses evil. None of the living humans were given such blessings, and it is for a reason."

"What reason?" asked Ali.

"You're the only hope for peace to be restored."

Ali resisted this idea in the beginning and decided to join the army, but after two months, he felt the obligation toward the entire earth to save it from Ceres' corruption. He never regretted this decision; on the contrary, following his cause was as easy as breathing.

While thinking of these memories, Ali fell asleep and woke up to the voice of Sai, who handed him a jar of water.

Ali drank and smiled at Sai, "How is your friend?" asked Ali.

"Good, we spoke a bit. He wanted to visit the Speakers. Are you ok with that?" replied Sai.

Ali agreed and reassured his companion that they were not very far from the Speakers' place, and Sai took the opportunity to ask some questions. He started by saying, "How do you keep this flame lit, pursuing this almost dead cause?"

Ali taped Sai's knee twice, "We don't have a choice. It's either that or being enslaved."

The Dharatian decided to share a thought he had never revealed to anyone, "Sometimes, I wonder if we're the bad people here. I mean, look at us. Every crime comes from one of the seven kingdoms: theft, lying, cheating, and killing. Meanwhile, people from the Union are busy with their occupation and they're progressing in every aspect," Sai expected Ali to be upset with this statement, but instead, he was smiling, and Sai continued, "Why are we revolting against them?"

Ali smiled, "On the one hand, you're not wrong. On the other hand, you limit yourself to appearances, which are misleading most of the time. Remember, when you're walking in a desert, sometimes you spot water on the road, and once you get there, there's not a single drop of it. It's just your eyes that mislead you.

The bottom line is never make a judgment until you analyze the situation from every angle. The thieves and criminals you see in the seven kingdoms were born in a corrupted system, and they were exposed to poverty and dictatorship, not to mention the prevention of learning; you can't expect them to turn to nobles."

"What about you? And Alighieri and Nora? Why did you all turn out better than noble people?" asked Sai.

"These are exceptions. You can't apply this rule on them. What about you, Sai? Why do you think you're different?"

Sai thought about what Ali had said and remembered how he used to live before meeting Roulan. He forgot everything his parents taught him, and was trapped in the world of crime. Sai realized if it weren't for his wife, he would have probably remained a thief or worse, and not everyone in his situation had a chance to meet a great person like Roulan.

Before sunset, they arrived at the Speakers' cave.

Chapter 14

Alighieri couldn't be happier , to be trusted by Ali. Being part of the rebels honored him, and leading them made him realize how far he had come in life. He always felt extraordinary, not for his courage or intelligence, but for his wisdom, which he thought he had gained from his mother. Genivra was her name. She spent twelve years as a servant of the Solum's queen. Her devotion and excellent service made the queen give Genivra her freedom to marry the man she fell in love with – a blacksmith who owned a small farm outside the city.

Genivra and her husband offered Alighieri a warm, lovely home and an excellent education. The blacksmith made him special with swords and taught him how to be a great fighter. His mother, however, showed him how to distinguish between evil and good; thanks to her, he learned that bloodshed is wrong.

He had killed once in self-defense, and the sadness he felt, made him swear not to kill anyone again. Even when the Solum's soldiers burnt his parents alive and took everything they owned, Alighieri didn't plot for revenge and isolated himself in a village and lived among them, where he fell for a pretty girl. When he was about to marry her, her family was ordered, by the king, to marry his brother the king who ordered her family to make her a bride for his brother, and she agreed.

This broke Alighieri's heart, and he decided to take revenge but wouldn't kill. Instead, he took something more valuable, which was the booty from the empire's soldiers. He spent three years setting traps and stealing from them.

Alighieri had never pictured himself as a thief. Instead, he had expected to become the king's advisor. Sadly, there was no decent king left to advise on earth, but the appearance of Ali and the rebels resurrected his hopes.

"A good leader doesn't exclude others from his plans." Nora interrupted Alighieri's thoughts.

As usual, Keita intervened with a joke, "He's probably thinking about what your face looks like when you sleep,"

Nora was offended but chose not to react, and Alighieri noticed, "Lady Nora, you're the only legitimate heir left in this world. Excluding you should be considered a crime."

Arsalan turned to Keita and said, "You see how men address highborn ladies?"

Keita lowered his head and apologized to Nora, who smiled at him.

"What's your plan, Alighieri?" asked Roulan.

Alighieri smiled and asked them to follow him, and they did. They reached a giant rock, and the farmer explained, "Behind this rock, I hid a lot of gold, which I stole from my corrupted kingdom and the empire. Consider it yours. I suggest we use it to hit the empire."

They were all staring at each other, perplexed, so he added, "What do you think?"

They all agreed to attack the barracks and kill as many soldiers as possible.

Alighieri couldn't hide his disappointment. Nora noticed, so she said, "Last time, you were the only one who was right. Your silence could have cost us our lives if it weren't for Roulan and Arsalan."

"Ali chose you for a reason to lead us, so speak your mind," added Roulan.

"My real enemy is Ceres and those who hold power in the council. Soldiers are just like slaves. They were brainwashed. Some of them are fathers. Killing them would make us as evil as Ceres," explained Alighieri.

Arsalan didn't like the response and asked sarcastically, "So you want us to kill Ceres and Ramessess ? Oh, how could we miss that? It is a hard idea to come up with!"

Alighieri realized that his Topraki friend was mocking him, so instead of reacting impulsively, he was cheerful and said, "My apologies Arsalan, I don't mean to insult your intelligence, but I just wanted to hit the empire badly. Not necessarily by killing their leaders.

"Do you remember how the emperor reacted , when Ali fooled him with the story of Ila? He sent his forces to kill 4000 men and women. This was a tremendous loss for us, but we have gained something precious; Ceres was exposed, and people started to see his evil side." Alighieri sighed and continued, "What if we sneak into the castle and hurt his pride by doing something bolder, like kidnapping a general or stealing a valuable thing from him? To provoke him!?"

Arsalan exchanged a look of admiration with the others and said, "Maybe Roulan was right. Ali chose you for a reason, but you will have to elaborate on that plan."

Alighieri stood and started moving among them and talking, "Have you ever heard of the Majesty? It's Ceres' sword, which he inherited from his grandfathers. Some said that its blade has existed for hundreds of years. The emperor is obsessed with it and loves it more than his daughters. He called the best craftsmen and blacksmiths to remake it the sword number one."

"I have heard many stories about it!" said Roulan.

"I have seen it, and trust me, I have never seen such a beauty. The pommel is circular, with a yellow diamond surrounded by tiny triangles, so it gives the shape of the sun. The gird was covered by leather in brown color and scattered with seven little diamonds that has d shades of the kingdoms. On top of it , is a cross guard made of gold; it has a rectangular shape and is pointed at the end, and its edges are thin and sharp. A gladiator can cut a rock with it."

"How did you manage to see it?" asked Nora.

"Because my father was one of the blacksmiths who remade it. And Ceres killed him and everyone who put his hand on it, to keep deluding people that it was a holy sword"

The five rebels loved the idea of stealing this unique weapon from Ceres, and all assumed it would turn the whole empire upside down. Alighieri volunteered to do this task himself.

When he was asked why, his response was, "Because I was appointed as a leader!"

"And how do you suggest doing it that?" asked Roulan.

"I'll pretend to be a merchant. With our possessions, I can easily have my shop there and improvise!"

"So you have no real plan?" asked Arsalan.

Alighieri smiled, "It's a risk I'm willing to take!"

Arsalan tapped twice on Alighieri's knee, then said, "In the absence of Ali, you're far more important than any of us. I'll go instead of you."

The Solumy felt insulted even though he knew his friend was protecting him and insisted on going. The other rebels also volunteered, and the argument was about to start, but Arsalan stopped it, "We all proved that we're not cowards, and none of us is better than the other. So if I insist on going, it's because I can fool people easily."

Keita was about to reply, but Arsalan interrupted him, "I was raised by my grandmother, a spiritual healer. She taught me how to read people's minds. I can use these skills to fool guards and infiltrate the royal residence!"

"And how does this mind-reading work?" asked Keita sarcastically. Nora and Roulan smirked.

Arsalan realized they were asking for proof and didn't mind showing a demo, so he picked a leaf and asked, "How familiar are you with the game Right or Left?"

"You mean the one where we should guess which hand holds the leaf?" asked Roulan.

Arsalan nodded and continued, "I will hide this leaf in one of my hands. Whoever can guess in which hand the leaf is, will win, and by winning, I mean he or she got the chance to choose who goes to the empire and steals the sword."

"I thought you were going to show us how you can read our minds?" Keita said.

"Patience Keita, I will not only read your mind but also manipulate it. I mean, I will force you to choose the wrong hand."

Keita laughed and shouted, "This is ridiculous!" Arsalan didn't reply, and Keita added, "Let's play."

Everyone was keen to see the embarrassment on Arsalan's face. Who would believe that such a skill existed? Even magicians had never claimed that, so Keita was the first to play. Arsalan hid his hands behind his back to place the leaf in one of his hands. He then showed both his fists and asked Keita to guess.

Keita went for the left, and when Arsalan opened his left hand, it was empty. Then he opened his right hand with the leaf inside.

"Don't get excited. Let's play once more!" shouted Keita.

They repeated eleven times, and the Grondy couldn't guess it even once, which intrigued the others. They all played many times, and none of them could guess it a single time! Nora was the last one to give up and asked how he did it, but Arsalan chose not to disclose anything until they all agreed that he was the winner.

The five rebels agreed, and a smile didn't leave the Topraki's face, until Alighieri reminded him he needed to shave his hair and beard because all healers are bald and beardless. Arsalan turned pale, and Keita didn't miss the opportunity, "You'll look like a rabbit when it's skinned."

The joke drove the Topraki mad, and he yelled, "You want a piece of me, Keita?"

"When you shave? Yes! I would love to have a piece of you," everybody laughed, including Arsalan.

The next day, Nora and Alighieri went to buy supplies, clothes, and medicines that Arsalan would need for his new job. Keita took care of shaving the Topraki's head and face. He promised he wouldn't throw any jokes, and he didn't, until the end when he could no longer hold himself back from describing Arsalan's head as an onion.

The humiliation didn't stop there for Arsalan. The girls used their cosmetics to make his skin whiter and tattooed his face with orange marks using a powder called Henna. He wore a white robe and a big necklace; he held in his right hand a long stick, and the worst part was his ride. It had to be a mule, like all healers.

His friends accompanied him to the forest and said their goodbyes, and Nora reminded Arsalan to tell them about the trick he used in the game.

"In reality, I had two leaves." Arsalan opened both his hands, and there was a leaf in each one. Then closed and opened them both simultaneously, and they were all perplexed to see one of them disappear.

"Where's the other leaf?" asked Keita

Arsalan raised his empty hand and moved his index slightly, and the second leaf fell away, leaving everyone surprised.

Keita shouted, "But this is not mind reading!"

"Yet, you believed me!" replied Arsalan with a smile. Then he asked his friends to not stay near the castle"

"Stay alive, my friend. We need you here," replied Alighieri.

Arsalan walked with confidence on the bridge. He was pulling a mule with two bags full of supplies. Two guards stopped him at the gate. He wished he could break their necks, but decided to focus on his new role. He smiled and spoke slowly, "May the Gods preserve the empire. We shall not worry when we have strong and smart men like you to guard it."

"State your name and why you're here?" asked one guard.

"My name is Eren, and I'm from the Kingdom of Toprak. I'm a healer and can read spirits, minds, and the future. I heard men like me are valued and treated well in your empire, so I come to offer my services."

The two guards looked at each other and laughed. One of them asked in a sarcastic tone, "So you can tell what will happen to us?"

"Yes, soldiers. For example, you both will have two gold coins each," said Arsalan and handed them four gold coins.

The two guards loved the man's attitude and welcomed him with a smile. One of them even showed him the way to the market.

Although Arsalan was in the army and from a wealthy family, he couldn't help but be impressed by the splendid and thick walls of the empire. But not as much as the military tactic they used to defend the castle. At the top of the wall were at least ten giant bells, each attached with a long cord which even a five-year-old child could pull in case of emergency. Next to each cord was a stairway leading to the top of the wall.

It wasn't over. While Arsalan was walking to the market, there were boxes made of cement on each side. Arsalan knew they were storage units for weapons since they had the same in Toprak. He finally reached the market – or the Souk, as it was called in the empire. Unlike all the ones he'd been to, it was very organized. The shops were grouped by the type of goods or services provided. He walked among the groceries first, then the fabric, where he saw many faces from his kingdom, Toprak.

When he reached the smithy, he couldn't help staring at the beautiful swords and daggers.

"How can I help you, healer?" a voice came from behind.

Arsalan turned and found a man in his fifties, bald with circle earrings. He was wearing a red robe. The Topraki was reassured to be called a healer, so he smiled and replied, "I need help, my lord. I'm new in your beautiful city and…."

The bald man interrupted, "Say no more. I know what you need: a shop, a place to stay, and access to food," he offered with a smile and continued, "We have pretty women from every race. You could be accompanied by a sixteen-year-old Topraki girl if you choose."

Arsalan thought of cutting the bald man's tongue, when he heard that girls from his kingdom were used for pleasing visitors. But he controlled his anger and turned it into a smile, "That's very kind of you. A shop and place to stay in would be enough."

The bald man suggested taking him to a hostel so he could relax and eat. As for the shop, he showed him a tent in the healer's submarket and promised it would be furnished and ready before dawn.

When they arrived at the hostel, Arsalan handed over the money for the shop, plus a gold coin as a tip to the bald man, who took them without hesitation and thanked him.

Arsalan added another coin, so the bald man would tell people about his skills. The man was excited and informed Arsalan that his shop would have a crowd bigger than he had ever seen.

CHAPTER 15

It had been two days since Ali left Sai and his friend, Advik with the Speakers. Ali had missed being alone, and now he was riding towards his companions, enjoying the greenery around him, and thinking about the future. He was very optimistic despite everything that happened: his new six companions resurrected his hopes to free the world from Ceres.

His thoughts were interrupted by a soft voice coming from behind. He turned quickly with his hand on the pommel of his sword, but he didn't fetch it. Instead, he stood petrified looking at something he'd seen before. A perfect combination of a human body, even though the dress indicated she was a lowborn girl and her face was covered with mud. It couldn't hide her features: she was tall and had messy brown hair, but she was still pretty with her sparkling blue eyes. A perfect straight nose and hearty lips adorned her face. She was holding a dagger with both her hands, which were trembling, "Where did you take my sister?" she said.

Ali took his hand off his sword, and before taking another step, the pretty girl shouted again, "Don't get any closer, or I will kill you!"

Ali realized how innocent she was, thinking she could kill him with a small dagger. He raised his hands and spoke gently, "My lady, I meant no harm. I do not know about your sister, but if you put the weapon down, I might be able to help you."

The girl didn't obey and yelled, "You all say things like that in the beginning!"

Ali could imagine what the girl had been through, so he fetched his sword and two daggers, put them down and said , "My name is Ali, and I'm from the Kingdom of Turba. I was raised to respect women and not harm them. Why don't you put your weapon down and tell me your name?"

"Heal is my name, but you're not fooling me with your sweet words."

Ali raised his tone. "My lady, you don't even know how to carry a dagger properly. I would have already hurt you if I wanted to!"

"Why should I believe you?" asked Heal.

"Because if I do harm you, maybe someone will harm my beautiful unborn daughter one day," replied Ali.

These words finally calmed Heal and made her drop the dagger, and she said, "Please, can you help rescue my sister?"

"I promise I'll help you."

Ali took his bag and fetched a tissue and a bottle of water. He threw them next to her, and she wiped her face first, then drank. After that, he gave her some bread, and she ate it.

"How come a highborn girl like you is wearing scruffy clothes and in a place like this?" asked.

She raised her head and asked, "How do you know I'm a highborn girl?"

"You cleaned your face before you drink." The girl stared at him, and he carried on, "The need for food and water is in our nature, while looking nice is something people acquire in wealthy families."

"Maybe male instinct, but females always like to look astonishing, especially in front of young knights. But you're right." replied the girl with a smile.

She told Ali she was from the Solumy kingdom, and her father was the prime advisor of the king. The Turban recognized her father as a traitor, but chose not to condemn his daughter.

The blond girl engaged in a conversation, and he filled her in with some of his life's events which impressed her, and she dared to ask him, "How come a knight like you isn't married yet?"

"Deep down, it's what I want most, but I have a more worthwhile cause. I want to offer the next generation-a better world," replied Ali.

"A world empty of the empire? Right?" asked Heal.

"Not really, my lady, only those who are trying to wipe the identity of the other kingdoms," said Ali and added, "But enough with me, tell me what happened to you!"

"My sister was married to a commander in the Kingdom Topraki. We were escorting her to her groom, and suddenly, bandits attacked and killed everyone except the women. They took us into slavery. I was lucky to escape and…" Heal couldn't continue and started crying. Ali didn't dare to open his mouth.

The following day, , Ali was preparing his horse, and Heal suggested filling their bottles from the river, which wasn't far. The Turban was trying hard to deny his feelings to himself. He had never felt like that before. Even his devotion to the cause started fading when he looked at her. He wished he could take her to another world, safe and empty, and live there eternally.

He lost himself in those joyful thoughts, but couldn't go further, as his ears caught Heal's screaming. He thought she'd seen a snake or something like that, so in no time he sprinted to the river, and to his shock, there was a man behind her, holding her neck with his forearm. From his uniform, Ali realized he was from the Union.

Ali stopped and did nothing except look. Ten other soldiers showed up. The man holding her finally spoke, "Drop your weapon if you want her to live."

Ali didn't and replied, "You clearly have a problem with me. Why don't you let her go?"

The man replied, "We know who you are. I'm not a fool to take that risk even with my ten men. Surrender, and she might live."

"I also know you, and I will not do what you ask. Plus, if you kill the girl, you will all die," said Ali confidently and added, "Since you know who I am, here's something that will reassure you. I swear on the name of the creator. If you give her a horse, I will surrender."

The Turbans were known for their devotion to the creator, and perjury was the last thing one would expect from them. The soldier holding Heal released her, and she sprinted toward the horse. Without even saying thank you, she galloped and disappeared.

Ali waited until she disappeared and kept his word. He dropped his sword and made no resistance. The soldiers couldn't believe they had the rebels' leader in their custody. They chained and tied him to a tree.

Ali was in a state of fatigue. His face was covered with blood as he threatened, "The minute we move from here, the deal will be off, and I will find a way to escape. Before that, I will kill you all!" he paused and then continued, "Unless you untie me, then I give you my word that I won't hurt anyone."

One soldier hid his fear and replied, "You can deal with our chief!"

"What chief?" asked Ali.

The chief didn't delay and showed up on the horizon with a uniform different from any soldier Ali had ever seen. As the knight approached, Ali couldn't see his face as he was wearing a helmet. All the soldiers knelt before him. He got down off his horse, went straight to his prisoner, and removed his helmet.

Ali was in shock. The only word that came from his mouth was, "Heal?"

"Leah, not Heal. I am Ceres' daughter," she said, "You're not the only smart one who can invert the letters of his name to fool the others."

The first thought that hit Ali's mind was an old saying. *"Never trust a woman."*

He didn't expect this sweet and innocent girl to not only be Ceres' daughter, but also a liar who took advantage of his decency to trap him. Still, he also acknowledged what she did, was brilliant – after all, they were at war, and he did the same thing to her father.

He smiled and said, "Bravo, you fooled and caught me easily. But here's a piece of advice, kill me because the longer you wait, the better chance I will hit back."

Leah smiled. "I'll take my chances."

Ali doubted that this innocent girl was as evil as her father, despite what she did to him, so he asked her why she wanted to kill him.

"I'm cleaning the world from people like you. My father is trying to build a better world, while you, the rebels, love to destroy everything beautiful. But it's over for you. There's no Eleah, no Isaac..." before she continued, she noticed Ali's face turned pale when he heard Isaac's name. She knew he must have been dear to him, so she pushed the pain harder. "I was the one who cut his head off."

Ali in a disappointed tone said, "How could you kill a powerless man like him? What was the crime he had committed to deserve an execution without a trial?"

"You can ask him yourself when you join him!"

Ali was very disappointed with Leah; he thought she might be different, but she was worse than her father. He opened his mind to every tiny detail to use for his escape, he was sure it existed, and he gained this can-do attitude from one of his trainers who had an expression he said to all his trainees, "*Even if your hands are tied and a sword is on your neck, you still have a chance to survive.*"

Only those with a sharp ear can fully understand its meaning. Ali was one of those. He was tied to a tree with a chain that had five lockers. One around his neck, two on his hands, and another set for his feet. The lockers were attached with a short chain, so if he released himself from the tree, he wouldn't be able to use a sword or run correctly. His only option was to reach the princess, surround her with his chain, and use her as leverage.

He didn't try to free himself from the tree. After all, they would have to leave at some point and do it for him. Not long after, Leah came next to the tree, trying to piss him off, "Seriously, what were you expecting from saving a random girl? Glory or gold?" Ali was about to reply, and she interrupted him, "Wait, maybe I could have fallen in love with you? Fool!"

She thought her words would upset him, but to her surprise, he smiled and replied, "My lady, I consider it a duty to save people – not just pretty girls like you. And you're partially right. I mean, something unusual happened to me when my eyes met yours."

"What a loser!" sighed Leah and ordered her soldiers to untie him from the tree so they could leave. Ali prepared himself, and the minute the cord was untied, he stood quickly and used his head to hit the first soldier in the face. Another one came with his sword. Ali kicked him with both his feet in the belly, and before the third attacker reached the prisoner, Ali had already placed his chain around Leah's neck. She tried to resist but felt immobile like she was paralyzed.

"Drop all your weapons, or I'll squeeze her neck," snarled Ali.

The soldiers were all scared and couldn't object to their enemy. They knew Ceres would slaughter them if anything happened to her, so they all obeyed and put their swords down.

"Here's what's going to happen. Whoever holds the keys will have to unlock my chains. After that, I will be given a horse and run with the lady until I'm safe, and I promise I'll send her back," commanded Ali.

One soldier thought Ali wanted to fool them and asked, "Why should we trust you?"

"Because you don't have a choice. Trust me, and you will return with your princess alive, don't and…" replied Ali.

The soldiers looked at each other, then at Leah. One of them fetched the keys from his bag and walked towards Ali, then Leah screamed, "Don't come any closer."

The soldier panicked and couldn't move, and Leah added, "He's just bluffing. He will never kill me." She then screamed the name of one soldier, "Rob, prepare your arrow and shoot on my command!"

Empire of Rebels: Rise of Rebels

Rob immediately placed an arrow in his bow and redirected it to Ali.

Leah whispered in Ali's ear, "You know, Rob can aim for the eye of a flying bird, so either you release me and look for another chance to run, or I'll order him to pierce your eye," then added, "Which one do you want in your grave, left or right?

Ali said nothing, and Leah ordered Rob to shoot on ten. Then she started counting. Ali was confused. He couldn't kill the girl nor surrender himself. He thought of squeezing her slightly to scare her, but he couldn't guarantee her life after that. Leah reached six. Still, another four numbers and Ali's life will end. At eight, he released the princess and raised his hands.

The soldiers picked up their swords and went toward him. They kept kicking him for a while and left him on the ground. Leah whispered in his ear, "Never confess your feelings to a girl."

Chapter 16

Arsalan's mother died when he was born, and his father followed a year later. Luckily, his grandparents were there and took good care of their grandson until he was sixteen.

By then, Arsalan had already joined the military service and reached a leader ranking in less than five years. He enjoyed his work and considered serving the Kingdom of Toprak a privilege that not anyone was fortunate enough to have. He impressed all the generals along with the previous king, and they didn't delay in promoting him to commander. Sadly, he didn't have the chance to enjoy his new role, as things started taking another direction, when the emperor Ceres deposed the legitimate king. Arsalan decided to take control over his life and left everything. This action cost him his family and could have almost killed his soul if it hadn't been for Ali.

Everything had changed for the Topraki. His ambitions had become a lot bigger than setting traps for entry-level soldiers.

He couldn't believe that he was sitting in a hostel a few hundred feet away from his enemy Ceres; he didn't care if he died as long as Ali and the other companions were alive. In the meantime, he was eager to reach the emperor's sword and take it out of the castle, looking forward to seeing the smile on Nora and Roulan's faces, the admiration of Alighieri, and the jokes Keita would throw.

Arsalan hardly slept and went to the Souk before sunrise, finding his new tent already furnished. He decided to add authenticity to his shop by placing twenty glass jars filled with liquid in different colors and hung parchments containing many drawings, like spiders and snail's houses.

Arsalan went out and started looking at the other tents which had different shapes and colors. At first, he didn't understand this variety of colors until the owners started coming to their shops. From their clothes, he realized that each one chose the color of his kingdom for his tent. He kept observing everything around him, and suddenly the bald man who had helped him the day before showed up.

The hairless man was smiling and walking toward his new guest, Arsalan. The bald man stopped among the healers' shops and started speaking loudly. "People of Union, our emperor offered the entire world the possibility to come to our Souk and expose their skills. It's a blessing for us to see people from other worlds making our lives easier using their talents, but today we have an exceptional guest.

"Eren is his name and he possesses a unique talent which even the Speakers themselves will be pleased to see. Eren can read minds and predict the future. Today he's offering his services for free."

Arsalan's shop became like a magnet. An uncountable number of people headed to his shop. He smiled and kept moving his head left and right, trying to find the victims who will undergo his first demonstration and taking advantage of his lipreading skill. Then a question came from the crowd.

"Are you a magician?"

Arsalan spotted the young man behind the question. The Topraki smiled at him and replied. "As a matter of fact, I am, but what I'm performing today is beyond magic. It's based on science." The Topraki marked a silence to intrigue his audience and continued, "In fact, our body exposes things we hide in our minds. I learned to understand how every part of our bodies speak," replied Arsalan and raised a parchment in his hand as proof that everything he was doing was based on science and not just magic.

No one spoke, and Arsalan asked "Any volunteers?"

Most attendees raised their hands, but Arsalan kept looking for a face he could easily read.

There he was, a man in his forties with frowning eyes and biting his nails. Arsalan spotted him begging his upset wife earlier, so the Topraki called him enthusiastically. The man couldn't disobey in front of all these people. Arsalan shook his hand and asked him about his name.

He answered, "Dan."

The Topraki put his index finger on Dan's forehead, closed his eyes, and said, "This isn't your name."

Some of the audience spoke loudly, "You're right!"

Arsalan ignored them and warned the man who lied with a smile, "You can either tell me your real name, or I will reveal an unpleasant secret of yours," then he turned to the attendees and continued, "We all have awful secrets…"

The man didn't hesitate to share his real name which was "Emile."

Arsalan kept quiet, and all the attendees were waiting for his next move. After a long silence, he spoke, "Emile, you're very frustrated today. I can tell it's not because of one of your three sons. I bet it's your…." The Topraki marked a silence, then continued, "It's your wife. She did something you didn't like, and you reacted like a storm. Now the anxiety is killing you, wondering if she would forgive you or not!"

"He's an imposter, don't believe him!" answered Emile.

Another voice came from the crowd, "He's telling the truth." Laughter filled the area because they saw Emile's wife confirming the mind-reader's claim.

Arsalan whispered in his ears, advising him to buy her jewelry, then noticed that somehow people started buying his bluffing, but still he wanted to reinforce this thought. He called a girl in her twenties, who looked extremely excited.

The Topraki closed his eyes, put his index on her forehead, and said, "Your name is Kate, right?"

The girl put her hand on her smiling mouth and nodded. Then Arsalan started drifting his index between her eyes, then under her nose, inviting her to keep looking at it. In the meantime, he started talking slowly, "Miss Kate, our eyes can fool us and make us see nonexistent things, like dreams and mirages. somehow, you were fooled by a finger, and now I'm commanding you to sleep." Then Arsalan counted to three and taped her forehead. Kate lowered her head and was about to fall.

Arsalan held her from her back and added "And here she is sleeping against her will,"

People, including the bald man, were petrified. The look on their faces showed panic, and Arsalan enjoyed that for a while then taped the girl on her left shoulder. When she opened her eyes, he added,

"Good morning, Miss Kate. Did you sleep well?"

The two acts were enough for the Topraki to build an excellent reputation in the Souk.

His shop was the most crowded one, thanks to his sharp eyes and ears which made his work easier. He spotted things quickly, and when he revealed it, he made it look like he possessed an invisible power. After three days, a big fish finally took his bait.

One general, who went by the name of Philip, was the chief of the treasury in the empire. Arsalan was informed secretly by one guard that Philip was interested in his services. To give some credibility to his work, Arsalan pretended to be busy, and a moment later, the same guard came and threatened the spiritual healer to close his shop if he didn't come at once.

Arsalan couldn't miss the opportunity and accompanied the guard to the royal residence.

The Topraki had heard many stories about the wealth of the empire, but had never thought it could be represented in walls instead of just gold and precious stones.

When he left the Souk, he couldn't believe his eyes when he started seeing the royal residence. Its walls were perfectly shaped as if giant swords had cut them; their orange colors were shining, and in the center was an oval brown gate, made of wood and gold. Two guards were standing there wearing black leather suits, with orange helmets, they were holding spears and didn't move.

The gate was opened and Arsalan entered a hall, with a giant fountain in the center surrounded by greenery and flowers in various colors and shapes.

A short man wearing a red robe and a white turban with an orange diamond in the center, walked towards the Topraki, He presented himself as the chief of treasury Philip.

Fortunately, Keita had briefed Arsalan about the manners of the Union, so he knelt and kissed Philip's left hand, "My lord, it's an honor to meet you, consider me your humble servant!"

Philip didn't smile back and replied, "We'll see about that. My guard will lead you to your chamber, and we'll speak tomorrow."

Arsalan was delighted to hear that he will stay in the royal residence. He considered it tremendous progress in his plan, as he was not so far from the emperor's sword.

The minute he crossed the residence door, he handed the guard two gold coins. The guard looked at him and asked, "What is this?"

Arsalan tapped his shoulder and said, "Thanks to you, I'm lucky to be in such a place, as not any healer can get in here."

The guard smiled, and Arsalan didn't wait to throw a compliment, "I assume you're no ordinary soldier? Being allowed in here isn't a privilege given to anyone,"

The soldier bought the compliment and boasted, "I'm a third-ranked soldier and my grandfather was a commander."

Arsalan finally asked the question he'd been preparing, "Is this the residence of chief Philip?"

The guard laughed and replied. "No, this is the royal residence."

This was good information for the Topraki, but he also realized how challenging his mission will be. When he walked past by each suite, there were twelve guards at the entrance; not to mention those who were inside, he assumed the security would be even higher in the emperor's residence. There was a lot of thinking to do before executing his plan.

Arsalan went to his room to sleep. He didn't wake up until he heard the knocking on his door. When he opened, a different guard came in with two young girls.

Empire of Rebels: Rise of Rebels

One of them carried a plate with bread, olives, and about a pound of barbecued meat. The guard said,

"Once you have changed and eaten your breakfast, I'll come back to escort you to Lord Philip."

Arsalan handed two coins to the girls, who both smiled, and one of them thanked him for his generosity. Later, she came back to Arsalan, who thought she was sent by Philip as a gift to please him.

"Not interested!" barked Arsalan and was about to close the door, but the girl blocked it.

"Neither am I," the girl said, "I'm a Topraki, we offer our bodies to a legitimate husband only!"

"And why are you away from your kingdom?"

The girl's eyes were filled with tears as she answered, "I was taken from my kingdom against my will. My father was a general, you would know him, General Ottoman"

Arsalan was shocked because Ottoman was his father's cousin, which made the girl from his blood.

She noticed the look on his face. "Yes, I was at your wedding. The little girl who held the candle next to Afet, your wife," said the girl smiling and wiping her tears.

"Aiyla? You've grown up since the last time I saw you, but your eyes haven't changed," said Arsalan and continued, "I need to get you out of here."

"I always doubted that you're one of the rebels, but now I'm sure. Carry on with your mission – you can rely on me to help you."

"But you're not safe here!" warned Arsalan

"For the time being, I am safe. My owner is Princess Leah, she would never let any monster touch me. Plus I'm Topraki, I can defend myself," replied Aiyla with a wink.

They carried on their discussion and Aiyla filled Arsalan with every secret she knew about the emperor and his generals.

After that, Arsalan was escorted to his new client. When he arrived, Philip ordered everyone to leave his chamber except for Arsalan. It was easy for the Topraki to read the frustration in his eyes. He looked like a teenager who'd fallen in love for the first time.

"My lord, I'm thrilled you trusted me with whatever you have in mind."

"You claim you can read minds. If that is the case, then tell me, Eren, why did I call you?" asked Philip in a firm tone.

"May I speak freely, my lord?" asked Arsalan.

"And quickly!" urged Philip.

"Your wife is having an affair, and you need my help to decipher the matter," replied Arsalan.

Philip turned pale, and words couldn't come quickly from his mouth.

Arsalan approached him and whispered, "Your secret is safe with me, my lord!"

Philip tried to hide his frustration and asked, "What do you need to reveal the identity of her lover?"

That was a golden opportunity for Arsalan to extend his stay in the royal residence, so he explained, "These matters are murky, and I need to be more than certain, my lord. I need at least three days!"

Philip seemed relieved and didn't have a problem with that, so Arsalan asked to have some freedom to walk inside the residence.

"Don't get closer to the emperor's suite or the dungeons. Otherwise, you're free to walk in the corridors."

The next day, Arsalan thought of every single plan, but none of them had the slightest chance of working. Like sneaking to the emperor's chamber at night, which was an inevitable suicide given the number of soldiers around.

He thought of pretending to be one of the emperor's chamber guards, but unluckily for him, the guards inside the residence didn't wear helmets. He knew he couldn't fool anyone with his face after his fame in the market.

His first day was a total failure, and the Topraki thought the second day would be better, but it was not. He woke up to the sound of the horns and drums. The screaming of people in the Souk penetrated the wall of the royal residence and reached his ears. He assumed it was a feast he wasn't aware of, so he quickly put some clothes on and left his chamber. One guard was running with a joyful face and screaming, "Princess Leah caught the traitor Ila!"

Arsalan didn't feel his feet and almost fell. He couldn't hide the shock on his face, then went into his chamber, and could hardly stop himself from screaming. Losing Ali was like losing the entire cause.

The Topraki locked himself in and let no one inside . He pretended to be concentrating on Philip's matter, but he was not. All he cared about was how to rescue Ali. He spent the whole day thinking about a plan with no success.

In the evening, he went to Philip and tried to take advantage of him. He was let in by the guards.

Philip was eating and didn't have the courtesy of responding to Arsalan's greeting. Instead, he asked without making eye contact, if he had discovered the lover's identity.

"My lord, I was making good progress and could narrow my research to eleven people…" explained Arsalan.

Philip dropped his fork and took a severe tone. "And?"

The Topraki continued, "Since this morning, my thoughts have been disturbed by this outlaw you caught. Being in the same residence is very disturbing to my soul and thoughts."

"What do you expect? He's his highness' prisoner," asked Philip angrily.

"A conversation with him would help me a lot in this matter. As he's a dead man, his spirits started moving around, so if I speak with him, I might be able to clear my head from them," replied Arsalan. He knew it was like gambling: either his ask would be granted, or he would lose his head.

Philip screamed, "Guards!"

The anxiety started getting to Arsalan, but he remained put. When the two guards came in, Philip continued, "Take him to the dungeon and leave him with the rebel until he's finished."

The two guards looked at each other and obeyed.

***

Ali was in his cell, feeling very disappointed to see his life ending so quickly and without seeing a glimpse of victory against his enemies.

Remorse was eating him from the inside; regretting his weakness toward the woman who tricked and captured him. In the meantime, he kept hope thanks to his six friends. Ali knew they wouldn't stop following his cause. He was thinking about each one of them, then interrupted by the guards unlocking his cell.

The rebels' leader thought it was another kind of torture, but when his visitor took off his hood. He felt like he had been resurrected from death.

"Arsalan, what are you doing here?"

"It's a secret mission, Ali," whispered Arsalan with a smile. He asked Ali the same question, but he didn't respond, instead, he laughed at Arsalan's new look, "I'd give anything to see the look on Keita the first time he saw you!"

Arsalan smiled back, "Imagine he was the one to shave my head and beard!"

"Tell me why you are here!" said Ali.

Arsalan filled his friend in with the entire plan of stealing the emperor's sword and Ali couldn't have been prouder of his companions.

"Don't worry, my lord. I will not leave this castle without you," replied Arsalan.

But Ali persuaded his friend to stick to his plan and promised he would find a way to leave the empire soon.

"I have a friend here, her name is Aiyla. I'll make sure you get my news," said Arsalan.

Ali smiled and said, "Best of luck my friend!"

Chapter 17

The three days were over, and Philip summoned Arsalan to his chamber. The treasury chief was standing with an angry face, and the Topraki knew he was dead whether or not he revealed the lover's identity. So he delayed the matter as long as possible.

"My lord, I have revealed the lover's identity," started Arsalan, with no introduction.

"Speak! What are you waiting for?"

"I might lose my head if I do, my lord. It's not something you want to hear."

"The one thing you will lose your head for is if you keep your mouth shut, so speak and don't test my patience!"

Arsalan lowered his head and mumbled, "I'm afraid it is his highness, the emperor."

Unexpectedly, no shock came to Philip. It was like he already knew. Still, he asked how sure the healer was.

Aiyla had assured Arsalan that she saw Philip's wife in Ceres' room several times, but the Topraki knew that if he confirmed the matter to the treasury chief, his life would be over. So he chose to be vague, "Not entirely, my lord,"

After a long silence, Philip said, "After all, you didn't help much."

Arsalan spoke immediately,

"If it was anyone else, I would have been certain, but his highness is no ordinary man. He was chosen by the Gods to rule the world; accessing his mind isn't as easy as you think," he felt he got the attention of the treasury chief and continued, "There's one way to be sure about that: if I can get my hands on something valuable of his highness!"

"Like what?" asked Philip.

Arsalan was reassured to see Philip buying this new lie, so he replied, "Something of great value. I mean the thing he loves most, like a horse, a sword, a special diamond!"

Philip frowned his eyes and asked, "That's an odd request!"

"It is my lord. Before coming here, I said the same thing to the spirits who informed me, but they insisted that I need something valuable," improvised Arsalan.

"I thought you're a man of science, not a magician!" asked Philip in an angry tone.

"Science can't be certain when it comes to great people such as his highness"

"Fine, I will figure something out, but it's going to be your last chance. Understood?" said Philip.

Arsalan knelt and said, "Loud and clear," then asked permission to leave.

The anxiety almost killed the Topraki – not from waiting but to know if Philip was playing him somehow.

Luckily Arsalan was wrong, because Philip came later to the Topraki's chamber with something hidden in a sheet. The General put it on the bed and uncovered it. It was the most elegant and beautiful sword he had ever seen. The treasury chief whispered, "This is the sword of his highness. He loves it more than his heir. Be quick! I'll have to return it as soon as possible."

Arsalan was scanning the sword, thinking what to do next. The sword was in front of him but sneaking it out of the castle would be a lot harder.

"What's wrong? If you don't succeed this time, I'll feed you to my dogs," Philip said, interrupting Arsalan's thoughts.

The Topraki realized that time wasn't helping, so improvising was his only option.

He placed his left hand behind Philip's neck and his right one on the chin, then turned until he heard the click of his bones, letting the treasury chief fall to the floor dead.

He covered the sword and used it as his stick, leaving the residence to the stable. No one could speak to him since he was a general's guest. Time kept pressing because Arsalan knew that the minute Philip's body would be found, it would be impossible for anyone to leave the castle. So he hid in the stable and to his luck, the soldier responsible for throwing the garbage came in to pull his horse. Arsalan jumped at him and slaughtered him before he made any sound.

A golden opportunity arose for Arsalan. He decided to wear the garbage man's clothes and helmet, then took the trash himself.

In no time, he fastened a horse to the wagon and attached Ceres' sword underneath, heading to the gate. Luck was at his side, no one stopped him, even when he reached the gate. The soldiers opened it with no question asked, and when Arsalan was about to leave the castle and taste an epic victory, a voice came from behind and screamed, "Wait!"

Arsalan stopped. It was a soldier wearing a leader's uniform, "What are you carrying?"

The Topraki tapped on the left side of his chest and replied, "Garbage, my lord."

The soldiers' leader came closer, fetched his sword, and started piercing inside the wagon. Arsalan understood it was a precaution against prison breaking.

The leader retrieved his sword, and while he was trying to place it in its sheath, he heard a sound down the wagon. Without speaking to Arsalan, he commanded one soldier to look below the wagon.

Arsalan knew it was the emperor's sword. At that moment, his death became inevitable. The soldier took the object he found and handed it to his leader, who in no time uncovered it.

The leader's face went into shock, and before saying a word, Arsalan quickly kicked him and took the sword. He used it to cut down two soldiers and ran. He was on the bridge, hoping to reach the forest alive, even though he knew it was impossible to run over a mile and survive all the arrows.

He kept sprinting, relying on the iron top and helmet he was wearing. No arrow could pierce him from behind. He crossed half of the bridge without a single drop of blood. He turned his face and saw at least twenty soldiers running after him. Their leader screamed, "Aim for his feet!"

Arsalan kept running, hoping the soldiers would miss as it was a tricky spot. Six arrows missed, but the seventh didn't.

He fell, and when he turned around, he saw all these soldiers coming toward him. He knew it was the end. Still, he broke the arrow in his calf and decided to die in honor and take as many men down as possible.

He rose to his knees, taking a fighting stance and waiting for the clash.

Suddenly, an arrow came from behind and pierced a soldier's neck, then three others. Arsalan turned his face, and a smile crossed his lips.

It was Nora and Roulan with their bows, then he saw Keita and Alighieri running from the left side of the forest with their swords. The girls released their bows and joined the fight, and in a matter of minutes, they finished twenty-three soldiers.

The Topraki asked Nora to shoot three firing arrows in the sky, and she did; it was a sign to Aiyla in the castle. She didn't delay taking the news to Ali.

The emperor hadn't got the news yet. He was enjoying the victory his daughter had brought him. Having Ali in custody was like an obsession for him, and now that the rebels' leader was locked in his cell, Ceres couldn't keep himself from visiting him with his daughter.

He badly wanted to aggravate his prisoner, who was lying down in his cell. Ali was looking forward to seeing the look on Ceres' face when he learns what Arsalan had done. His wish was granted, and both the emperor and his daughter came to pay him a visit.

From their ecstatic look, he assumed they hadn't learned the sword's news yet, and said "I must be lucky. Not every prisoner has the chance to be visited by his highness and the beautiful princess."

The emperor used the same tone and replied, "You're an exceptional guest, Ali. Or shall I call you Ila?" Then continued, "I must confess, you're a very smart man."

"You remember the last time we met, you promised to give me one of the five holy names? Will you keep your word?" asked Ali.

Leah decided to jump in and shoot back, "Why does it matter? You're a dead man!"

Ali smiled and redirected his sight to Ceres, "Am I?"

The emperor seemed to enjoy the exchange and replied, "Yes. And because you're an enemy I admire, I will make sure your death will be celebrated every year."

Ali finally found the moment to deliver the heavy news but chose to do it delicately, "I assume that I will have the privilege to be executed by you. Won't you use your beautiful sword to do it?" Ceres exchanged a look with his daughter, and Ali added, "You don't seem to be aware of what's happening in your castle, yet you call yourself an emperor! While you were having an affair with one of your general's wives, a friend of mine stole the Majesty and got away!"

Ceres laughed loudly and replied, "I thought you're a smart man, but using this move to fool me, makes me doubt it."

Ali remained calm. "There's only one way to find out!"

With no further words, Leah sprinted to her father's chamber. While Ceres and Ali kept playing the word game, Leah came back with a pale face, "Father, the Majesty isn't in your chamber, and Lord Philip was found dead in one of the guest rooms."

The big bell started ringing, which confirmed all what Ali had claimed. Ceres couldn't hold himself back and fetched his dagger, but Ali only smiled. "If you kill me, the Majesty will be buried and will never see the light."

"How dumb are you? We wouldn't trade you even for an army!" said Leah.

"That's very flattering Princess! But your father isn't as smart as you think. After all, I think he values the sword more than you and your two sisters!"

Ceres said no more and left the cell. Leah addressed an angry look to the prisoner and followed her father.

Ali couldn't be prouder of his companions, and for the first time since Leah arrested him, he could sleep with no anxiety or worries about his life.

As for the emperor, he went straight to the council's chamber with his daughter and convened all the generals. Leah had never seen him in such a state. With red ears, a pale face, and frowning eyes, she could tell that the rage inside him could destroy mountains.

The nine generals came in no time. They were standing and waiting for their emperor's command, who finally ordered them to have their seats. He asked the new military chief, Vlad, to enlighten him on the recent theft.

Vlad couldn't raise his head. He spoke with a shameful tone, "Your highness, he pretended to be a healer. Somehow he fooled Lord Philip into getting inside the royal residence."

"And how could he get his hands on my sword?" asked Ceres.

The military chief hesitated initially, then replied, "The soldiers saw Lord Philip carrying something covered with a sheet from your chamber. It was the same sheet the soldiers found in the wagon he was trying to escape in."

Ceres clutched his chair's arm as if he wanted to squeeze it until it breaks. "And how could one man leave the castle's gate with over twenty soldiers on his tail?"

The new military chief couldn't reply, and the emperor started yelling, blaming everyone in the empire.

No one could speak except for Leah, who stood and, in a firm tone, said, "Father, for now, there's only one priority. Get back your sword." She turned her eyes to the generals, "This is the symbol of our power. Losing it will weaken our reputation, and the rebels' ideas will be promoted in the seven kingdoms."

She got their attention and didn't stop, "Father! Like I brought you the rebels' leader, I promise to bring you your sword."

The discussion continued, and they all agreed on entrusting the mission to Leah. The first thing she did the following day, was to give a visit to Ali, who was offered for the first time something to eat. His mood was ecstatic, and his mouth broke into a broad smile when he saw his visitor.

"You look better today!" began the princess.

"It's not every day I get the chance to see your father pissed off!" Ali shot back.

Leah knew how good he was in the game of words, so she decided to switch to something more dramatic. "Why did you spare my life the last time? You knew it could have cost you your life, and you did it anyway."

"Have you ever heard the saying: *once bitten, twice shy*?" asked Ali while Leah stared at him. "You're sly. In other words, you pretend to care to win people's trust, so they can open up and reveal what's in their hearts to use it against them. I must confess, it worked on me the last time , that won't happen again!"

Leah smiled and replied, "I thought I asked you a question!"

The smile on Ali's face disappeared and turned into a serious look. "You were not expecting an answer. You were trying to wake up the good side of me, and use it against me like before, but pay attention, as a man, I can't hurt you, but my beautiful friends Nora and Roulan would take pleasure in cutting you in half."

Leah used the same tone to reply. "You think you're the victim here. Your friends had just killed twenty-five men!"

"It's you who started it, and what's coming next is a lot worse."

Leah decided to cut to the chase. "What are your terms for giving us back the sword?"

"Isn't that obvious?" asked Ali.

Leah replied with a question "how can I trust your word?"

Ali laughed loudly. "We both know this should be your last concern. I saved your life twice. If I were you, I'd start thinking about how to pay back my debt."

Leah didn't add a word and left his cell.

It took her four days to convince her father of her plan, which was to go alone with Ali to fetch the sword from the rebels. She reassured them he was a man of his word.

The following day, Leah prepared her horse, and another one for Ali after he was unchained and given proper clothes.

Leah was confident that her enemy wouldn't turn against her, and that idea disturbed her. Deep down, she admired him for being a decent man, but she also hated him for causing all these troubles to her father who she loved more than anything in this life. He was not only a good father and a great ruler, but also the mother Leah didn't have. He took good care of her. When she grew up, he nominated her to be the heir to the Union empire, until her baby brother would come of age.

When she visited other kingdoms, she realized how great the Union was. Unlike the seven kingdoms, there was no poverty, and no crime. All this was thanks to her father, who not only built the empire from scratch ,but also was trying to make the other kingdoms better places. That was why she hated Ali and his friends: because they were ruining what her father was trying to build.

Ali interrupted her thoughts, "When we arrive, my friend and I will have to look for another place to hide in."

Leah grimaced, "I can't understand you rebels! You choose to hide like rats instead of living like normal people."

Ali hesitated, thinking about the way he should speak to her.

Most of the time, he thought she was like her father, and therefore he had to be cautious with her. Other times, she seemed like a decent girl, who was a victim of her father's brainwashing. As Ceres was a robust politician. He hit the kingdoms with their own people and used his puppets to do the killing. At the same time, his proclamations of diplomacy made people believe he fought for justice. He convinced most of the Speakers to move to the Union, so every young man with an ambition to learn would have no choice but to come to the empire. He dominated the economy; therefore, all the businesspeople and craftsmen chose the Union as their home.

Ali chose to reply sincerely, "My lady, it's in the human nature to look for safety and run from starvation. There's nothing we want more than having a stable life like yours!"

"Then why don't you?" argued Leah.

"When dignity is taken away from you, nothing else has a taste. The dynasties who ruled for centuries were wiped out by your empire, and our traditions were stomped out like they were diseases. Even our clothes don't please your father, and he's obliging us to change them. I choose to die a thousand times rather than being a slave!" replied Ali.

The debate continued for half a day. Once they had ridden into the forest, Leah spotted five knights ready to shoot their arrows!

Ali asked her to relax and explained that they were his friends. After greeting them, he introduced Leah.

Nora advanced toward her and said, "Ali, say the word, and I'll cut her head off."

Leah said nothing, but Roulan did. She raised her sword and said, "Nora, for what she has done, you'll have to fight me for this privilege."

Ali lowered Roulan's sword and said, "Ladies! Leah made a deal with me. We'll give her the sword, and she will walk away."

Keita, Arsalan, and the girls didn't like Ali's proposal and started complaining, but Alighieri interrupted, "Folks, the sword is useless to us. We made a point. I mean, Arsalan humiliated them by infiltrating their residence. Isn't that enough?"

Roulan went close to Alighieri and said, "I don't care about the damn sword. She's the daughter of the man behind every crime committed against our kingdoms."

Ali didn't like the behavior of Roulan and decided to take a higher tone. "My friends, we made a deal, and she honored her part. If we don't hold ours, we're no different from Ceres."

Leah didn't say a word and was just observing, and once she laid her hand on the sword, the Union's soldiers started showing up from the trees.

Nora screamed, "It's a trap!"

The six rebels ignored the number of soldiers and went into a fight against them.

Arsalan was still limping, so he chose to stick next to a tree trunk and use his ax to defend himself.

Roulan used a sword in her right hand and an arrow in her left. Whoever missed her sword cut, she used the arrow to pierce him.

Keita had no shield. All he needed was one hit, whether with his sword or fist.

Nora was holding two swords and was enjoying cutting the soldiers down. The same went for Ali and Alighieri.

Arsalan was cornered by three soldiers and was struggling. He could hardly defend himself. Roulan was the closest one to him.

She started running towards the Topraki, but everyone doubted she would reach Arsalan alive. Still, she kept running, and all of her friends were just watching.

Arsalan dropped his ax. The four rebels were watching their friends about to die and couldn't do anything.

Suddenly a shadow appeared; quicker than a tiger when it jumped on its prey. The knight cut down the three soldiers in a blink of an eye.

Roulan finally stopped screaming, glad to see her friend survived the attack and scared of what she had just witnessed. She seldom saw people fighting as good as this knight, and it was her enemy, Princess Leah.

Arsalan's friends ran towards the survivor and started checking him. He was in a tired state but not wounded.

Leah interrupted, "He's still recovering from his last wound. He needs to relax."

Ali couldn't hide his admiration and said, "Thank you for not disappointing me, princess."

She got on her horse, and before leaving, she addressed Ali. "Isaac was a decent man, I didn't enjoy killing him."

Nora interrupted, "But you did kill him!"

Ali addressed an angry look to Nora while Leah replied, "He was sentenced to torment; an execution preceded by a lot of tortures. I disobeyed the whole empire to offer him the quickest death."

The princess got on her horse, and before leaving, she added, "Lord Ali, you spared my life twice, so I still owe another one."

Chapter 18

When Leah came back to the castle with her father's sword, she was furious and planning to face him for not being a man of his word. He had made a deal with Ali and didn't honor it; not to mention risking his own daughter's life to win back his dignity.

But she knew how smart he was, how he would easily escape her prosecution with his eloquence. She even predicted the kind of excuses he would use, "This is war, there's no place for emotions."

It's not that she didn't believe the statement, but some politicians like her father used it inappropriately to mislead people.

Leah wouldn't hesitate to trick her enemy in war, like she had done with Ali; she identified his goodness as weakness and used it to arrest him. She wasn't proud of it, but she didn't regret it either, and she somehow admired what her other enemy Arsalan did in stealing her father's sword.

For Leah, such trickery could be explained by the context of war, but when giving a word to someone, only indecent people break it.

Leah decided to lie, telling her father that the rebels killed all the soldiers and spared her life in the hope of a truce with the empire. She was hoping to distance him from Ali and his companions, who only showed great values. Deep down, she knew Ceres wouldn't do that.

At night, Leah's sleeping troubles came back to her again. It took years to recover from the nightmares she used to have.

It started when she was ten. Her father brought healers from every corner in the world, they knew many spells and potions to help her get rid of these awful dreams.

Leah didn't share with anyone the nature of the dreams she was having, choosing to lie and say they were ordinary dreams, like monsters coming to eat her. Given her age, everyone believed her, but in reality, her mother had always been part of her dreams.

Although Leah had never seen her, she recognized her in the dreams: a tall white woman, with long black hair and brown eyes. Her father killed her mother every time in the dream; sometimes he cut her neck, and other times he burned her alive.

She spent three whole years distancing herself from him, but when she recovered and finally revealed the real nature of her dreams to one of the Speakers, he explained to her that these dreams were from the devil who was trying to separate her from her father.

This time Leah chose not to share anything with her father or any Speaker in the castle. She instead decided to speak with Rio, a humble gardener, and a wise man.

Leah thought of going to his house but didn't want to draw attention to him, preferring to wait until his working day.

She woke up early and waited for him in the garden. When he arrived, he waved and smiled at her. Of course, he didn't dare to approach and talk to her, but she raised her hand and asked him to join her. After she insisted, he sat on a chair in front of her. She handed him a cup of juice made of strawberry and orange, and he couldn't refuse it.

After finishing his mug, he wanted to stand, but Leah warned him gently, "I didn't ask you to leave."

In a hesitating tone, Rio asked, "Am I in trouble, my princess?"

"I wouldn't share with you my favorite drink if you were. You're a good man, and I'm seeking your advice."

Rio looked surprised, and Leah poured juice for the second time into his mug, "I know you would say you're not worthy, because you don't have enough wisdom, but all I need are your thoughts."

Rio looked at her with a smile, and she went with her first question.

"What do you think about dreams?"

Rio replied enthusiastically, "Dreams can be one of two things: a disturbing nightmare or a vision. People before us discovered that our ears, eyes, and nose store everything they come across during the day, and at night our mind can use these events either to trouble us or predict the future. Sometimes we can see a distant past."

"How can a mind see things that haven't happened?

Rio picked an orange, handed it to Leah, and asked, "What would happen to this orange if we put it in a room and forgot it for months?"

"It will spoil, the color and the smell will change."

Rio smiled and said, "Bravo, my Princess. Thanks to your previous knowledge, you could predict the future of this orange. That's how our mind works during our sleep. It uses everything our senses acquired during the day to predict the future. Ancient people said that the past can reveal the future."

Leah didn't let go and asked another question, "And can't we do that when we are awake? I mean predicting the future?"

Rio got more excited, "No, because our mind is distracted, unlike when we're sleeping."

Leah seemed to follow and went with another question which Rio expected, "How can the mind see a past it has never witnessed?"

"I knew you would say that," replied Rio with a smile, "Our mind can connect us with other minds, either of living or dead people."

Leah understood it was a spiritual explanation, so she didn't really buy it. Yet she asked one last question, "How can we distinguish between a vision and a nightmare?"

"People before us said that a nightmare comes after the sunrise, while vision occurs before."

Although Leah wasn't a spiritual believer, the idea shook her because she remembered that every time she woke up from a nightmare, it was still dark. While she was thinking, Rio suggested to her, "My lady, there's one place where you can have more explanations about dreams."

Leah was intrigued, and Rio filled her in.

The following day she decided to pay a visit to her best friend, Sofia, the previous military chief's daughter. She hadn't spoken with her for months since her father, Peter, was executed by the emperor. His family was ordered to leave the royal residence and Ceres allowed them to inherit all the possessions of Peter and offered them a house.

Leah was ashamed to see her friend Sofia. Her servants told her, she was holding grudges toward the emperor, and the princess decided to give her time to digest the tragedy.

Things got worse when the emperor ordered the execution of Sofia's mother for inciting his guards to poison him. Leah decided to visit her friend, giving her the right to be mad at her too – after all, Peter was loyal to the empire his entire life, but his neglect cost him his life.

The princess expected an aggressive reaction from her best friend, but the minute their eyes met, they both couldn't hold back their tears. They hugged each other like old times.

Leah apologized for the late condolences and explained it was because she'd been ashamed of her father's act. Sofia was surprised and pleased to hear that Leah's love for her father didn't blind her, and they spent the entire morning chatting about everything.

When Leah told her friend about her nightmares and what Rio had suggested, it wasn't hard for Sofia to persuade the princess to go to the place the gardener suggested.

The following day, Leah and Sofia dressed up in soldiers' uniforms, sneaked out of the castle, and rode for three days to finally arrive at the Blessing Tree.

They recognized it from its shape and the marks written there. Rio told them to hold hands around it and think about happy memories. They fainted when they did, when they woke, it was hard to tell how many hours they had been unconscious. They were feeling dizzy and had a bitter taste in their mouths.

A voice spoke, and both of them thought they were hallucinating until the dizziness wore off . They were scared and kept interrupting the voice many times until the voice screamed and commanded them to silence.

The voice asked Leah to approach the giant rock and place her hand on it. Upon touching the wall, the place around her had changed.

A strange place that looked like a cell in prison. It was full of excrement and urine, but there was no smell, and although there were snakes all over the place, none approached her. She started walking backward and expected her back to hit the dirty wall, but it didn't.

Instead, she went to another dimension, with a green land and a clear sky.

The beautiful tweet from the birds made her forget about the disgusting cell she had just visited. She stood, started looking around, and observed a man with a long white beard on the horizon. When he approached, she thought he was her father, but he was much older. Leah dared to ask, "Who are you?"

"Your great grandfather," the old man said, "And I'm here to answer the question about your past."

"I know my past. I'm interested in my mother and my nightmares."

The old man smiled and replied, "Your mother is a part of your past, isn't she?" Leah said nothing, and the white-bearded man continued, "I assume you were told that your origins are from outlaws and criminals who were condemned to spend their lives in cells like the one you just visited?"

The old man didn't wait for her to deny or approve. He instead decided to give her the authentic version of their history, "You were once a great kingdom called Aqua; it was filled with decent people who prioritized peace and were trying to build a better world. Your skills and perseverance awoke the jealousy of some kings, so they decided to conspire against your kingdom and destroy it. The few of your people who survived these attacks spent their life running and hiding in the mountains.

He continued "Their descendants founded tribes and learned how to live in the shadows, until your grandfather and father came and founded their empire."

Leah was shocked by this new version and dared to ask, "So you're saying that Ceres has the right to destroy the seven kingdoms?"

"I'm telling you what happened. It's up to you to judge!" replied Leah's great-grandfather.

The old man disappeared, and a female voice called her from behind. When she turned, she recognized her. She was the same woman who kept coming in her dreams, and a strange feeling touched her heart. This was the woman who carried her nine months in her belly, supporting all the sickness and pain, eager to see her child coming into the world.

Leah couldn't hold back her tears. Her heart was pumping, she wished she could freeze the moment and keep looking at this beautiful woman. The only word that came from her lips was, "Mother."

The beautiful lady smiled and replied, "You should be proud of yourself. Only pure hearts are allowed in here."

Leah couldn't stop crying and said, "I would give anything to have you back, mother."

"You have a beautiful life ahead of you, my love. Choose it wisely, and you will have children who will fill the hole I left in your heart," replied Leah's mother. She changed her tone to one full of sorrow, "Darling, you have a beautiful mind and clean soul. Start looking at things with your mind, not just your eyes."

Leah remembered being told the same advice from Isaac in her dream and started crying.

"Killing Isaac was a mercy to him. Only decent and brave people can do such a thing," reassured Leah's mother.

The princess felt glad her mother could read what was in her mind, and added, "I didn't have a choice, he was my father's enemy."

Leah's mother raised her tone. "Your father is an evil man. Do you know why he killed me? Because I gave birth to a girl and not a boy."

These were the beautiful lady's last words. Leah was crying when she woke up next to the blessing tree. Her friend Sofia was lying beside her, and Leah was scared that her friend was dead, but she wasn't. The princess woke her up, and they both returned to the castle.

After a long ride, Sofia couldn't stop herself from being worried about the princess' silence, so she dared to ask her what happened there in the cave.

Leah chose to answer her with a question. "What would you do if you learned that someone you deeply care about is an evil person?"

Sofia could read between the lines and knew that Leah was referring to her father, the emperor. Although there was no one she hated more than him, she chose to be objective and give the right advice to her best friend,

"It's a hard question, and it will depend on your strength. If you can stand against this person's evil, do it. If not, step aside, and don't help."

Leah spent the entire trip thinking about her friend's advice, whether to stand against her father and seek justice, or step aside and watch him turn the other kingdoms upside down. And for what? For crimes committed by their great-grandfathers a thousand years ago.

The other thing that was eating her from the inside was her mother's murder going without revenge.

The idea of killing her father frightened her even more, as he was the father any girl would dream of. He was always there for her. Politics didn't stop him from telling her bedtime stories every night, having breakfast with her, teaching her hunting, and sharing his wisdom with her. But now that she knew he murdered her mother and thought men were worthier than women. Her feelings towards him were twisted, she couldn't love him or hate him, but she knew time would help her clear this dilemma.

Chapter 19

A beautiful pigeon was stepping on the grass. Its neck moved along with its legs in perfect harmony. The bird went with its beak, giving the impression it was looking for something to eat, but it didn't grab anything. Its eyes were beautiful. They were brown with a black iris in the center, and the pigeon's neck was covered with green feathers getting thicker underneath with an ombre gray color.

Keita was advancing toward the bird slowly. He succeeded in not attracting the attention of the pigeon. When he got closer, he turned to Alighieri and Roulan, who were laughing. Keita looked at them and put his index finger on his lips, and when he was about to jump on the pigeon, a voice came from behind.

"What are you doing Keita?"

Without turning, he recognized whose it was and although he had enormous respect for Ali, he couldn't stop himself from complaining,

"Ali, you just cost me a delicious breakfast!"

"In some kingdoms, killing this bird is a crime punished by death," replied Ali

Keita was perplexed and asked, "Why? Does it know how to cook?"

Everybody laughed, including Ali, who explained, "People called it a homing pigeon. They carry messages from far away." Then he started mimicking the sound of the pigeon which came towards him. He grabbed it gently and fetched from its right leg a small parchment that was attached to it.

After reading it, a smile crossed his lips, and he didn't hesitate to share its content, making Roulan jump from joy. The letter came from her lover, who had been away for weeks. Ali explained that Sai's training was complete and that he would rejoin them in less than a week.

Ali added that Sai changed his haircut and that it was no longer cut from the sides. Keita didn't hesitate to joke, "This news is a lot better than killing Ceres."

Arsalan addressed an angry look to the Grondy, and so Nora who said, "Have some manners. He's our friend and Roulan's husband."

Roulan smiled and replied, "I agree with Keita. I always hated his haircut."

The rest of the group laughed, and all agreed that Sai's haircut had been awful. The discussion was extended to other subjects, and delight was on everyone's face. Knowing that Sai would join them with Isaac's skills made them hopeful again for their cause, although they had no idea what to do next, because they placed their trust in Ali.

The following day, Ali was sitting next to the river expecting his friends to join him discussing the new plan. The sound of trickling water mixed with the bird's tweets made him drown in his thoughts, thinking about Leah; the girl who did everything to make herself an enemy to him, but instead, he felt weak whenever he saw her. Ali couldn't let his heart take control over his life and ruin his cause.

When he'd been trying to forget about Leah, she intervened and saved Arsalan's life, killing her own three soldiers. Ali realized that his gut was right, and her heart was as good as his friends.

Ali stood when he saw his friends coming toward him and started speaking when they sat down. "We're the seven people who chose to carry this world on their shoulders. What we have done so far has shaken the seven kingdoms and the empire. I will not do the same thing this time by designing the plan myself. We're doing it together!"

He kept looking at each one of them and was pleased to see the joy on their faces, so he decided to address Nora first. "Nora, what do you suggest?"

The Token girl was surprised and didn't say a word, and Ali reassured her, "Say whatever comes to your mind."

Silence covered the area for a moment, until Nora realized she had no choice but to speak her mind. "We need to think bigger. Enough with setting traps and killing entry-level soldiers. What we need is an army of men and women ready to give their lives for a shred of hope to taste a world empty of Ceres. Of course, this army doesn't have to be equal to the emperor's. Remember, Ceres has defeated seven kingdoms with a tribe of fewer than 4000 soldiers."

Alighieri didn't seem on board, and reminded Nora that the emperor was lucky. He said that in the past, the seven kingdoms hadn't expected any attack, unlike the current situation where the empire was not only expecting Ali and his friends to attack, but also chasing them everywhere on earth. Nora was about to reply, but Roulan went first.

"Why Ceres and his father were the only ones able to reverse the balance in the Union's favor? How many leaders before them dreamed of having that? Every solution seems silly in such a situation , but we have to choose one and go for it, so for me , Nora is suggesting the right thing!"

"I agree, but we need a practical solution, not a suicidal one. Let's assume you were able to gather ten thousand men, do you think they could stand against hundreds of thousands of well-trained soldiers?" replied Alighieri.

Roulan didn't hesitate to shoot back, "Have you forgotten that Arsalan, Nora, and Keita took over three hundred soldiers in one day? Do you have any idea how many we could take with a thousand warriors?"

"It's not about the numbers, Roulan..." Alighieri trailed off.

Ali interrupted, "Alright folks, she spoke her mind, and so should you."

Keita was the next to talk, "I agree with Alighieri, we need a place to host an army."

"Not even that," replied Alighieri, "Let's say we were able to bring ten thousand well-trained soldiers to a safe land. What about their food, weapons, housing, nursing?"

Ali remained quiet and stared at Arsalan, who smiled and said, "I don't think I will be able to come up with brilliant ideas like these, just consider me as your loyal soldier."

"How humble our spiritual healer is!" said Roulan in a sarcastic tone.

Arsalan found himself cornered, and knew they wouldn't let him go until he spoke. "Well, none of you are wrong, but before raising an army or looking for a land, we need supplies and everything the people will need."

Nora found what the guys said ridiculous and wished Ali would intervene. But he was just smiling.

"What are you expecting from me?" asked Ali.

"Speak like everyone else," Roulan replied.

Ali stood and said, "I've nothing to add, all the plans seem good to me. I'd like to consider them all."

"How will we achieve our goal, while we disagree with each other?" asked Alighieri.

"Each one of us will do what he or she suggested. I mean, Nora and Roulan wanted to raise an army, Arsalan and Alighieri would like to prepare the supplies and needs for this army, and Keita is interested in finding a safe land."

Nora looked at Ali," So Roulan and I will look for volunteers to join us?"

"You bet. Keita and I will try to find a safe land. As for Arsalan and Alighieri, they will take Sai with them to prepare everything our people will need."

They were all excited to start their new responsibilities, and keen to see their seventh companion. Of course, not as much as Roulan who was very anxious. As the week passed, and Sai hadn't arrived yet, she thought of sharing her concerns with Ali, but hesitated to avoid worrying him.

The following night, while she was sleeping, she had a disturbing dream; Sai was in the execution yard, his arms were both cut and blood all over his chest. Several soldiers were raising their swords to kill him, but Princess Leah was standing in their way, defending him.

"Roulan, Roulan! It's just a dream!" Nora screeched, waking up her friend.

"Something is wrong with Sai, I need to find him," said Roulan.

"It's still night, wait until the sun rises. We can all go with you. I promise." replied Nora.

Nora did her best to prevent her, but couldn't. When they both left the tent, they saw Ali laying down next to a tree. He stood the minute he saw them.

Nora ran to him and said, "You need to stop her, she's worried about Sai."

Ali didn't reply and went straight to Roulan, holding in his right hand a piece of paper. His face was pale, and his tone was hesitating. "Roulan, I need you to sit down."

The way Ali talked and the paper he was carrying implied one thing; something happened to Sai. The tears started falling from her eyes, and she asked a question she never thought she would ask, "Is he dead?"

"No, he's not, but he's in the emperor's custody."

It was like someone took a dagger and started piercing her heart. She quickly imagined the love of her life chained and being tortured as she saw in the dream. She started screaming. Nora hugged her, and all her friends were watching in total panic.

Ali couldn't tolerate the state of Roulan because he felt responsible for Sai's arrest. He went next to a tree and laid down, as he knew that in such a state, he wouldn't be able to think clearly. He spent the whole night in the same place, feeling guilty, but he took an oath to himself, he would bring Sai back to his wife.

The following day, he went to Roulan's tent and asked permission to enter. He had a shameful look on his face, and eyes full of tears . Ali spoke in a soft voice, "You have every right to hate me. Sai has been arrested because of me, but mark my words, I will bring him back safe."

Roulan stood and replied, "shame on you, Ali. Do you think I blame you? You're risking your life for everyone on this earth. It's the emperor I hold responsible, not you."

Ali was relieved, and so was Nora, who asked him how their friend had been arrested.

"His friend Advik sold his soul to the emperor and exposed our plan," replied Ali, then addressed Roulan, "Roulan, the six of us will work on a plan to rescue him, and we'll definitely figure something out."

Chapter 20

After the execution of the previous military chief, Peter, Ceres hired one of his cousins; he was known by the name of the Terrorist, and his real name was Vlad. A man with no mercy in his heart and a thirst for bloodshed. His job was managing the Hell; a dungeon used for torturing outlaws.

In the current circumstances, Ceres saw him to be the right fit to fill the military chief position. For Ceres, he was the only man able to shut down the potential rebellions inside the Union.

One of Vlad's first tasks was to extract information from the new prisoner, Sai, the man on whom all rebels' hopes lay. Sai had spent a month and a half doing nothing but reading parchment left by Isaac and conducting experiments. He succeeded in achieving many results, but the one he loved most was the powder he made from some rocks and plants. His idea was to mix it with clay and make bricks which would be used to build the walls of their new home. While he was preparing to join his wife and friends to start delivering,

Empire of Rebels: Rise of Rebels

his friend Advik exposed him to the empire's soldiers who arrested him and put him in the Hell.

Sai thought he'd be executed like Isaac, and it didn't scare him. He had no regrets and was sure that Ali would find another rebel to carry out his work. The painful hole felt in his heart was for Roulan, the woman who changed him from a pathetic thief into a great man who would die for the most significant cause on earth.

After two days in prison with no food, Vlad decided to pay a visit to Sai, who wasn't scared of him despite his look. He was a giant man with a belly, his eyes popping out of his face, and he had one tooth missing from his mouth which was surrounded by a red mustache.

Vlad unlocked the cell's door and initiated with a question "How come your skin is so brown? I bet it's from your dirty blood."

Sai ignored him completely, and Vlad held him by the neck and squeezed it. The Dharatian resisted and showed no pain, then Vlad released him and said, "One thing I can assure you, you're going to die. The question is, how fast? And that, my friend, depends on you."

Sai couldn't keep his mouth shut, "You know, it's in the human nature to show compassion and kindness, but life's circumstances change people and make their hearts like stone. I have to confess, I seldom meet people with your hatred and aggressiveness. Which makes me wonder why you're so on edge," Sai stopped and noticed a surprised look on Vlad's face, so the Dharatian decided to push harder, "Usually this kind of behavior is the result of a tragic childhood. I'm sure you were not beaten, I'd say it was worse than that."

Vlad held him by the neck again and threw him on the wall, "We'll see if you can keep this enthusiasm tomorrow!"

Sai realized , he will soon be praying to die.

***

Not so far from Sai's cell, Ceres was in his room expecting his prime advisor, who had just returned from his new kingdom and didn't delay joining his emperor. Ramessess got worried when he saw Ceres' state, pale and unable to hide the sadness from his eyes. The prime advisor knelt and said, "Your highness, you don't look well. Should I call a healer?"

Ceres invited him to sit. "Three healers have checked me and found nothing. It's all the thinking that has gotten me in this state, Ramessess,"

"And what could possibly disturb you, your highness?"

The emperor grimaced, "Everything. My daughter is no longer the girl I raised; a rebel got inside my residence, killed a general, and stole my sword. Of course, it didn't stop there. I just learned that they found a replacement for the mastermind." Ceres raised his tone even higher, "Are we becoming weak, Chief Ramesses?"

Ramessess bowed before his emperor again. "Your highness, I know why you called me, rest assured, I will do whatever it takes to get it done!"

Ceres stood and went next to Ramessess, "I want Ali, dead or alive! The rest is meaningless to me. You have my authorization and support to do whatever suits you to achieve it."

"I won't disappoint you, your highness," said Ramessess sand left straight to Vlad's residence.

On his way, he kept thinking about the new mission, and for the first time in his life, he wasn't sure of fulfilling it.

He'd rather chase a demon than Ali, the fearless man with a mind sharper than anyone he'd ever known. Ramessess was the only general who agreed with Ceres, that the whole empire should be mobilized to catch Ali. Luckily for Ramessess, he held a precious asset of Ali, and he chose to use him as leverage to catch the rebels' leader.

He arrived at Vlad's chamber, who welcomed him enthusiastically and invited him for lunch. Ramessess didn't say no, grabbed a wooden chair, and sat beside him. The tables had three plates of different types of meat, two fruit baskets, and two jars, including one filled with strawberry juice.

They talked about some regular subjects related to the military, and when they were done, Vlad suggested taking the discussion to the garden. While walking in the greenery, Ramessess finally cut to the chase and asked, "What are your plans for the new prisoner?"

Vlad grimaced, "If only his highness gave me his blessing to kill or even torture him."

Ramessess smiled and tapped Vlad's right shoulder. "We need Sai alive and safe to trap Ali."

Vlad turned red and exploded, "Why should we give all this consideration to a pathetic rat like Ali? Wasn't he just a slave here?"

Ramessess replied in a calm tone, "It's his highness' command."

"No, I'm sure it was his daughter's suggestion! And it's a shame to have women involved in politics?"

"Do what you were told!" concluded Ramessess and took his way.

The prime advisor understood why Vlad was angry. The military chief enjoyed torturing his enemies, and Ceres prevented him from this pleasure, because he was aiming for a bigger fish; trading Sai for Ali. They knew the rebels' leader would be embarrassed in front of Roulan and his other friends. The prime advisor had kept a few pigeons of Ali which he retrieved from the Speakers' cave, so communication with the insurgents was easy.

***

Once the bird arrived at the rebels' camp, they all gathered around the tree where it landed. They had to wait, until Ali came to grab the letter attached to the pigeon's leg.

While Ali was reading it, his face turned pale, and he tried to mislead them by saying, "They wanted to trade Sai for the gold Alighieri stole from them. I think it's a fair deal."

It was a blatant lie to all of them and unexpectedly, in the quickest way, Roulan retrieved the letter from Ali's hands and ran. No one followed her, and she stopped a few feet away. When she read it, she looked at Ali and screeched, "You want to trade yourself for Sai!"

The other four all turned to Ali with a look of shock. He didn't speak, but Alighieri did, "I badly want Sai in the group. He's a crucial member to us , not to mention, he has a wife, but it's a game the emperor is playing."

Nora also decided to intervene. "There has to be another way. Let us work together on a plan like we always do."

Ali finally spoke. "There's nothing to plan. I spent years in the Union and I have friends there, so I have higher chances of escaping than Sai."

Roulan was trying to hold her tears, "Ali, Sai is everything to me, and I won't say no to trading yourself for him. But remember, you don't have to do it. No matter what happens, you'll remain my chief, the one I follow until the last day of my life."

Ali could imagine the pain she was going through. On the one hand, she wanted to follow the same path as her friends; on the other hand, she wanted her man next to her to grow older with .

***

Ali had to find a good trading plan quickly. He was sure, his friend Sai was in a lot of pain, and he wasn't wrong, except it wasn't physical but rather a mental one. As Vlad was commanded not to touch him, so he chose to make him watch the most awful torture he'd ever seen. The soldiers brought a young man, took his clothes off, and attached him to a cross. His feet and hands were tied apart. Vlad came with a curved dagger and used it to cut the manhood of the young man, whose screaming filled the whole place. And to stop the bleeding, Vlad placed a glowing blade. The young man fainted from the pain. Vlad did this to three other young men, and every time, he threatened Sai he would do the same to him.

The Dharatian couldn't sleep at night. The scream of the three men didn't leave his ears. He had never witnessed such torture. Still, he wasn't tempted to reveal his plan to survive, and was ready to go through that pain or even a higher one, rather than putting the cause he stood for in jeopardy.

While immersed in his thoughts in the middle of the night, he heard footsteps coming closer to his cell. He thought it was Vlad coming to mess with him, but to his surprise, it was not. Sai stood and looked out of the bars. He saw a guard and another person in his company. He couldn't tell who it was, but clearly not a soldier, as he was wearing a robe with a hood that covered half of his face. A few feet away, the hooded person stopped, and the guard continued and unlocked the door, then left.

The other visitor decided to reveal his face, and to Sai's surprise, it was a pretty girl.

"May I have a word with you?" initiated the girl.

The sound of words was soft and implied kindness, but Sai decided not to fall for the bait and replied in a firm tone, "Do I have a choice? Who are you?"

"My name is Leah. And I am ...." But before she completed her sentence, Sai exploded in her face,

"How dare you come here after what you did to Ali?"

"This is war, Sai. Do I have to remind you that you've killed hundreds of us?" Leah replied in a calm tone, but not Sai. He raised his tone higher.

"You wiped out our economy, traditions, and beliefs, and you're trying to cleanse us. What do you expect in return?"

Leah kept her tone calm and said, "I'm not here to place the blame or address insults. I'm interested in a simple chat, and I swear I mean no harm to you." Sai didn't reply, and she continued, "I met Roulan. She seems like a decent woman, and I can tell you're a good match."

Hearing his wife's name shook Sai's feelings, and he couldn't help but to smile. "I disagree. There's no match for Roulan. No man could fill her greatness!"

Leah smiled, "You're lucky to find each other. Go and live far away from this ugly game of politics!"

"You think love is enough in life? I can tell you it's not. Love is like a flavor that makes you enjoy whatever you're doing, but it does not solve all problems," said Sai.

Leah asked sarcastically, "How does being a rebel taste?"

"Rebel is just a word you labeled us with. We follow a man we believe in justice who doesn't care which kingdom rules. To him, the good is his kingdom, and enemy is his the evil. He lives for others, fighting injustice and making the world a better place."

"Isn't that utopian? I mean you keep facing danger, but what good are you getting from it?" asked Leah.

Sai could understand Leah, because he'd thought the same thing the first time Ali suggested joining him.

"There are no words to explain the reward we get. The only way to understand it, is to try it."

"I hope you'll reunite with your wife soon," replied Leah and left his cell.

Chapter 21

Ali had received a letter from Ramessess with a proposal.

"From The prime advisor Ramessess to Ali the rebel,

This conflict is between us, Sai has nothing to do with it.

If you want him back in his wife's arms, all you need to do is surrender."

Ali wouldn't hesitate for a minute to sacrifice himself for his companions, but he suspected that Ramessess was trying to fool him. In the meantime, Sai's life was at stake, so he wrote back to Ramessess requiring Leah to manage the trade.

A response came within two days, stating that his terms were accepted.

Ali started preparing his horse to head to where the trade will take place.

Roulan had mixed emotions, anxious for her husband and guilty because Ali will risk his life for Sai. She couldn't do anything except cry. Arsalan and Keita were trying to calm Roulan, and Alighieri was getting briefed for what was coming next.

As for Nora, she went away to the forest, avoiding to say goodbye to Ali, the man who made her feel secure. He was like her new family, giving her hope she might someday rule her people, like her father had promised.

Nora knew that if Ali died, the cause would die with him. Her heart told her, he was the only man on earth capable of bringing dignity to the seven kingdoms. She heard a noise behind her and knew he was coming to say farewell. He stood a few feet away and addressed her, "I'm honored to know a princess like you. I'm sure that one day, you'll sit on your father's throne next to your son, who you'll name after me."

Nora looked at him and whined, "Our cause will die without you!"

Ali came closer and said with a smile, "And who said that I'm going to die? I have a plan."

Nora knew he was trying to calm her down, because he was the kind of leader who shared everything, and since this time he didn't, she knew he was walking to his death sentence. But she couldn't object and decided to say a proper goodbye to him.

Before Ali left, he reminded her, "Remember, you're a queen. You're meant to be served."

Nora's state made Ali feel guilty, a brilliant girl who was meant to rule part of this world, placing all of her hopes on him.

Nora wiped her tears and followed him, "I will come with you for the trade.".

Ali smiled and said nothing. He rather walked towards his friends, having no idea how he could stop her. But he would never risk her life or anyone from his friends.

When they arrived, Ali froze in his place, unable to explain what his eyes were witnessing. Roulan was hugging Sai, and his three other companions standing with delighted faces.

Ali extended his sight and saw Leah standing alone, leaving him agape.

He advanced toward Leah and said, "Thank you for bringing Sai and trusting me. I will go with you to surrender myself."

Although Ali knew what it meant, he was glad to see the princess. Not only because she had held her end of the deal, but also for trusting him and his companions.

Before Leah replied, Nora fetched a dagger from her boot and ran toward her, aiming for her neck. But the princess was quicker and grabbed Nora's wrist before it pierced her neck. The princess fetched her sword and redirected its pommel, aiming for Nora's head because it was the only way to calm the Token girl.

To Leah's surprise; Nora wasn't as easy as the princess presumed. She fetched another dagger and blocked the princess' blade, and hit her in the nose.

Before it went further, a scream filled the area, "Nora, enough!"

They both stopped, and Ali carried on, "She held her end of the deal, and it's our turn to honor ours."

Nora yelled, "What honor do these murderers have?"

Arsalan added, "She's right. They were the ones who kidnapped Sai in the first place."

Keita agreed with Arsalan but not Alighieri, and they kept arguing until Sai decided to speak, "And who said she's here to take Ali?" an immediate silence dominated.

Leah looked at Nora with a smile, and Sai continued, "She went behind her father's back and freed me for nothing in return!"

The princess looked at Ali and said, "We can call it even now!"

Before Ali could reply, Roulan interrupted, "Princess Leah!"

She then walked towards her and hugged her. Leah looked surprised and did the same thing, then the Turang held the princess' right hand and mumbled,

"You might call it even with Ali. He saved your life twice and you saved his two friends. But me? You returned the love of my life to me, and for that, I'll owe you a huge debt."

Leah smiled, and so did the rest of the rebels. Nora approached the princess and said, "Don't expect me to say sorry!"

Leah ignored her and addressed the rest, "I did what I did, because Sai and you are good and decent people. But it's my home and father you're standing against. I know they're on the wrong side, but I decided to step aside and be neutral. I mean, I will no longer support my father, but I won't go against him either."

No one could reply, and Ali finally was able to speak, "Princess Leah, we appreciate the effort. It wasn't easy to do such a thing, and we respect your decision. Please take good care of yourself."

Keita turned to Arsalan and Alighieri, whispering, "I think he's in love with her."

They both smiled and chose not to reply.

When Leah left their camp, the joy returned, and Keita didn't hesitate to make his usual moves. "Ali, you never interrupt a girls' fight."

Roulan stood with a threatening look. "What's that supposed to mean?"

Arsalan replied, "He's right. It's a rule. You never interrupt a girls' fight."

The rebels carried on the discussion, and Ali reminded them of their roles. Nora and Roulan would go to the Dharatian kingdom. Their mission was to take advantage of the shaken situation and bring as many people as possible. Sai briefed them about everything in his kingdom: its streets, customs, habits, and a few of his old friends who could help. It would have been easier if he could have joined them in their mission, but he had a bigger fish to fry.

He was crucial to Alighieri and Arsalan's quest, which consisted of bringing everything they would need for their new land. As for Keita, he suggested going to one of the remaining tribes from his kingdom Grond and asking for a piece of land. The mission was extremely hard. Some would have considered it impossible, so Ali decided to accompany him. And after agreeing with everything, they went to sleep, but Ali couldn't. He kept thinking about the princess and her courage, and he was also worried about her.

***

Although Leah was Ceres' daughter, Ali knew that people like the emperor would sacrifice anything to keep his power and pride. He wasn't entirely wrong, because when Leah arrived at the castle, she felt some tension in the royal residence, and she went straight to the council. Without asking the guards, she pushed the door with her two hands and entered.

Ramessess went straight to her, "My lady, we were worried about you. We thought the prisoner kidnapped you and left."

Leah ignored him and continued toward her father who hugged her and added, "I'm delighted to see you safe darling."

"Father, I want to speak in private with you," proposed Leah.

All the generals looked surprised, but couldn't disobey their emperor when he raised his hand, asking them to leave the council at once.

Leah still had a shred of hope, that her father was a good person despite all the things she had discovered about him. She was hopeful she could persuade him into changing his politics and let the kingdoms live the way they wanted.

"Father, in the last two months, hundreds of soldiers were killed in this war by the rebels. That means hundreds of women were widowed, and many children were orphaned. Isn't it time to put an end to this?"

Ceres turned red from anger and replied, "If I didn't raise you myself, I'd say you're dumb or insane. The rebels attacked these soldiers on their duty. I won't leave these insurgents without punishment."

"We should probably ask ourselves why they're doing this? I mean, you can't deny they lost thousands of their men, and they have no control over their kingdoms," replied Leah, knowing that it would make him angrier. He raised his tone even higher and spoke, "They're savages, and without us, they'll bury each other alive . I'm doing them a favor by ensuring their protection."

"What kind of protection? Killing their scientists and craftsmen? Stealing their gold? They were living in peace until our empire came to light!" Leah replied, and before her father spoke, she lowered her tone and said, "Father, no one can love you like me, and I'm worried about you. We have everything in our empire. Why don't we leave them alone? If they're like what you're claiming, so be it. Let's live in peace until my brother grows up, so we can ensure our dynasty will last."

The emperor realized she was under the influence of someone, so he lowered his tone and replied, "Darling, politics is not that simple. Do you think they will leave us alone if we do?"

It was Leah's turn to raise her tone. "These are lies you tell yourself so you can sleep at night. I've read history, and for centuries trusses were maintained between these kingdoms until your father appeared. Don't insult my intelligence by lying to me, Ceres."

The emperor decided neither to speak nor listen to her, instead, he raised his hand and slapped her. Her right cheek turned red and her upper lip started bleeding.

She addressed him with a fierce look and before leaving the council, she decided to break his heart, "I'm ashamed to be your daughter. I know everything about you: I know you murdered my mother and corrupted the Speakers. You have no mercy, not even for your children, and from now on, you're an enemy to me."

She enjoyed the look of shock on his face, so she continued, "And you know what, Ceres? I'm the one who sneaked Sai out of the castle and killed the soldiers you sent to murder Ali, after you struck a deal with him,"

She then left the council, and the minute she entered her room, she heard a knocking on the door behind. She thought it was her father coming to calm her down, but when she opened the door, it was the last face she wanted to see. Vlad. She immediately addressed him with an angry look and asked him to go away.

He laughed and said, "I'm not here as a guest. I was sent by his highness. From now on, you're ordered not to leave your chamber. If you need anything, you shall ask the servants. I'll make sure the door is well guarded."

"Are you done?"

Without hearing his answer, she ordered him to leave, but he couldn't keep his rudeness to himself and said, "You're a shame on this empire."

At night, she was conflicted and wondered if facing her father with the truth had been the best idea, and somehow regretted it. Still, another voice inside her kept reminding her that what she had done was the right thing.

She slept and didn't wake up until someone knocked on her door. She knew it wasn't one of her servants because they were usually granted access to her room without permission.

She got up and put her robe on, then opened the door. It was again the disgusting face of Vlad. She immediately opened her mouth with a threat, "If you knock on my door again, I'll cut your hand."

Vlad smiled and replied, "I would never dare, if it wasn't important."

He clapped, and two soldiers came with a big wooden box.

He opened and retrieved a head from it. Leah put both hands on her mouth and screamed. Vlad enjoyed the look on her face and decided to push further. "Some servants saw you with him. We investigated and learned he was the man responsible for all these poisoned ideas, so he got what he deserved."

Leah kept crying for the person she admired most in the castle; for his sweet stories and great advice. The man who remembered her mother and shared many stories about her.

Rio, the smiling gardener she could never forget, was dead. Leah held her anger inside her, used the sleeves of her robe to wipe her eyes out , then said, "Mark my words, Lord Vlad, I'm the one who's going to end your life," then slammed the door in his face.

Chapter 22

It had been three days since Nora and Roulan left the group for Dharatee. The closer they got, the more Nora was impressed by such a place: there were no hills or mountains, but flat, green lands , with rivers , making the view breathtaking. The smell of vanilla was indescribably beautiful. Sai told the girls that the Dharatian's lands were once deserted. His ancestors relied on the gold mines .They had to live, using their fortune in the beginning to buy everything: fabrics from the Topraki; food from the Turba; and animals like sheep and cows from Token.

With the struggle its people had with the logistics, and the dependence on the other kingdoms, one of their kings decided to take another direction by attracting brains from all over the world to find him a better alternative.

These beautiful minds didn't fail him. They were able to plant and cultivate the deserted lands, raising animals, and succeeded in making their realm one the wealthiest and most beautiful places on earth. It attracted merchants and scientists from all over the world.

This remained for centuries until the Union came to the play, when the Kingdom of Dharatee went through the economic crisis , as a result the poverty made people forget all of their history and glory.

Turangies were neighbors of the Dharathians and suffered the same fate as the Union. Some of these memories came to Roulan, when she spotted the road that led to her kingdom. She didn't remember how their crisis started, but her mother had told her everything.

Roulan was born in one of the wealthiest families in Turang. Her father was a general and the king's brother. She was born in the royal residence and spent her entire childhood with her cousin, princess Li. They both wanted to be ladies like their mothers, and the thing they hated the most was the training fights. Both of them considered carrying a sword to be a boys' thing.

Sadly the appearance of the Union turned this great kingdom upside down, killing her uncle, the king, and his family.

Roulan's father played it politically, and didn't intervene in Ceres' plan, trying to keep his place as a general. But not Roulan. Losing her cousin Li changed her completely.

At the age of fourteen, she took sword training seriously and learned all the arts of fighting secretly. She never revealed it to anyone, even to her father, until the day her people were utterly humiliated in their own kingdom.

It was in one of the celebrations Turangy's king made to honor Ceres as a guest. One of the Union's leaders challenged all the Turangies soldiers to aim for a bullseye target, three hundred feet away. No one could shoot as good as him, and whenever he won a challenge, he would throw provocative jokes at the Turangies. Roulan was sitting next to her father, who wasn't very far from Ceres. The arrogance of the soldiers' leader didn't provoke her much, but what Ceres said did. "Turanguis' men fight like our girls."

Her father scoffed at Ceres' words, dismissing them as mere idle talk. But Roulan could not contain her frustration and stormed onto the stage where the soldiers' leader was boasting. "Is there any man left in Turang with the courage to defend its honor?"

The leader's expression changed to one of surprise as he caught sight of her, "A woman? Surely this must be a joke."

Roulan met his gaze with a steely determination. "The true joke would be losing to a girl."

The crowd erupted in laughter, and Roulan felt her heart sink as she saw her own people mock her. But she refused to let it discourage her, and challenged the leader, "Are you afraid?"

The leader said nothing. Instead, he placed an arrow in his bow and shot it, giving the impression of a casual shot, but the arrow landed dead center in the bullseye. He looked at Roulan with a smirk, "Impress me with something better."

"That was a mere half-inch from the center," Roulan retorted.

Whistles and jeers rang out from the crowd, but Roulan ignored them, determined to show them what she was capable of. She removed her shoes, moved backwards and stood on her hands. The noise from the crowd died down as they watched in awe as Roulan held a bow with her left foot's toes and an arrow with her right. She adjusted her body into the shape of a scorpion about to strike, raised her head slightly to spot her target and with a graceful movement opened her right toes, sending the arrow flying in a straight line to pierce the red dot in the center of the bullseye.

Everyone was stunned, including her adversary. He found no words to save his embarrassment. He raised his hand and said, "She's the best I've ever seen," but he couldn't support the humiliation and continued, "If only she had clean blood, I would have married her."

Roulan had always planned to avenge her cousin one day, but she was always worried about her father and mother. So she kept waiting, and when her family rejected Sai as a husband, she ran away from her kingdom and forgot entirely about revenge. All she wanted was to raise a family of her own. She was lucky to have her first child a year after her marriage, when he was killed, he took his mother's heart with him. Then all she cared about was bringing justice to her son and her cousin Li.

"What are you thinking about? Sai again?" the voice of Nora interrupted her memories.

Roulan turned to her, "Would you blame me for that?"

Nora couldn't reply because she had never been in love, she only loved her family and her new companions.

Roulan decided to tease her, "Are you in love with Ali?"

Nora pulled the reins of her horse to make it stop and yelled, "No way!"

Then lowered her tone and continued, "I mean, I admire him like you all do. Besides, the man is insanely in love with the princess."

Roulan laughed. "You're not as innocent as I thought. You could spot that?"

Nora liked that Roulan saw the same thing and asked, "Wasn't it obvious?"

Roulan sighed, "Well, I was concerned that you're into him. It wouldn't be easy to love without being loved."

Nora reassured her friend and told her, that her feelings for him were more of admiration. Then reminded her ,they had a bigger fish to fry, infiltrating the colonized kingdoms and convincing people to join them.

They both were aware of how challenging their mission was.

Roulan suggested trying with Dharatians first, because they suffered all forms of oppression under the empire. Unlike the other kingdoms, which were still living in the illusion of fake peace, they could earn their living in their own lands. Although all the businesses belonged to the empire, but who cared?

As long as they made profits, they could also send their children to learn in the Union free of charge. As for traditions and history, they no longer cared about that, and the Dharatians envied them and considered what they had as a luxury, given the new system Ramessess applied. In other words, all their businesses were frozen. No one was allowed to do any activity, the Union's soldiers were in every street, and Dharatians were told it will remain in this state, until the rebels were arrested.

Roulan wanted to take advantage of this situation and persuade people to join her cause. Their first challenge was to enter the kingdom.

The two girls looked nothing like Dharatians. Nora was white with brown hair and green eyes. As for Roulan, she was tall, which was unusual for women in Dharatee; her hair was cut short like an eight-year-old boy. Her eyes were big and narrowed from the sides, their black colors went with the color of her hair.

The Dharatian however were brown-skinned, and it was prohibited for a woman to cut her hair. So Nora and Roulan didn't consider the option to enter as guests, otherwise, the eyes of the Union would follow them wherever they went.

After a long reflection and discussion, they had an idea, which was to take advantage of greedy men's weaknesses.

They wore scruffy and torn clothes and sat at the side of the roads. Their plan was to attract soldiers who love to take advantage of weak women. They both knew it was a guaranteed option for most of men.

Empire of Rebels: Rise of Rebels

The first man who spotted them was a man in his forties. He was a soldier from the Union, he stopped and fetched a blanket from his horse's bag and told them. "Cover yourselves with this, it's cold!"

They stared at each other surprised, and the man added, "If you get inside the kingdom, you might spend the rest of your lives as slaves. March south, and you will find some abandoned cabins. I wish I could help you more," and took his way.

Nora and Roulan were touched and realized that even in the Union, there were still decent people. They didn't wait for long before two other soldiers appeared. The joy on their faces seemed like they had found a treasure.

One of them got down from his horse, pretended he cared, and spoke, "What's wrong, ladies? Are you lost?"

Nora replied without waiting, "Our husbands were mean to us, so we escaped with the hope to find knights worthy of our beauty and youth."

Nora looked at Roulan, and they both smiled and replied simultaneously, "And it seems it's our lucky day."

The two soldiers couldn't hold their delight and suggested taking them to the castle. They promised to treat them like highborn girls.

In a spoiled tone, Roulan spoke, "And can you get us in?"

One of them replied with confidence, "Of course, we can. Who can stop the Union's soldiers?"

The first challenge was fulfilled. They were in the castle of Dharatee, offered a chamber, and had access to a hot shower and nice clothes.

They both felt some regret for doing it. Being in the same room with a man was a sin in both their beliefs.

The two men entered their chamber expecting an unforgettable night with two pretty women. One of them approached Nora, raised his hand and redirected it toward her cheek. Nora immediately grabbed his hand, went with a sharp piece of glass to his neck, and pierced it. He fell on the wooden ground, making a noisy sound that caught his friend's ear. When he saw what Nora had done, he turned to Roulan with his hand on his sword, but the Turangy didn't let him fetch it. She grabbed a dagger behind her back , and cut his throat.

"What shall we do?" asked Nora, with blood all over her face and hands.

Roulan pulled one soldier next to the other and replied, "First, we're going to clean ourselves and wait until midnight. Then we can sneak these bastards out."

The plan went exactly as they wanted, and the following day, the castle square was filled with hundreds of people seeing something unusual. Two dead soldiers on the ground, their foreheads were written with blood, "The empire will soon fall."

Roulan was surveying the view in the middle of the crowd. She wore one of the soldier's suits with a helmet. Nora couldn't do that because of her height, which might be suspicious. Instead, she wore a man's clothes, and she used mud to change the color of her skin. It didn't look perfect, but the hood she wore helped her look like a Dharatian with a skin sickness.

Two nights later, they killed three soldiers and threw them in the same place.

The Union's commanders turned the place upside down. In the meantime, Nora joined a group of women who gathered daily in the garden to kill time. She took the risk and approached some of them, and to her surprise, most of them were pissed off and ready to do anything to survive the oppression of the empire.

As for Roulan, she played it big. As a guard, she took advantage of their prisoners' situation on her shift. She revealed her identity and promised to free them in return for helping her to kill the Union's soldiers. No one could refuse such an offer, as they all expected their execution within the next few days.

The two girls met every night in their chamber and briefed each other.

The following day, one of the Dharatians was going to be executed. He hadn't been tried yet, but the new circumstances obliged the commanders to make an example to the people of Dharatee, hoping they would be terrorized.

Nora was among the crowd watching the guards pulling the detainee to the execution yard, he was so scared, he wet his pants.

The Union commanders started speaking, "People of Dharatee, this man was found guilty of treason. He's the one who incited other traitors to kill our soldiers: the ones who were here to protect you. Now I sentence him to die."

Nora got off the crowd and went to a place, where she hid a bow and twenty arrows. Before the swordsman cut the detainee's head, she shot a first arrow which went to the executioner's chest.

The commander turned and saw the attackers standing about three hundred feet away, he screamed, "Seize him!"

Thirty soldiers started running towards her expecting she would run away, but she didn't. Instead, she kept shooting, and she launched six arrows without missing.

After that, she retrieved her sword and dagger and kept waiting for the clash. She could never take that number on her own, but she was expecting company.

More than a hundred women showed up from the alleys with knives, daggers, and sticks; some of them were carrying stones, throwing them at the soldiers who were utterly terrified.

Nora advanced and kept cutting them. Sadly many of these brave women bravely gave their lives, but the rest succeeded in killing the soldiers.

The commander ordered the remaining one-hundred soldiers to attack the women, and before they started running. They felt a vibration in their feet as the screaming began. The rough voices indicated they were not women, but instead, prisoner men led by Roulan with swords and axes; their number was huge, and in a matter of seconds they finished all the Union's soldiers.

The screaming filled the area, and Nora went to a woman and asked her to release all the homing pigeons to cut the communication. Roulan placed two of her new friends at the entry gate, ordering them not to let anyone leave the castle.

"Loud and clear, my lady," the two men replied enthusiastically.

Then Roulan joined her friend, Nora, who stood in the execution yard and started speaking. "People of Dharatee, you have seen today how we defeated these bastards, with women who never carried a sword in their lives, some of them died bravely standing against the enemy. They gave their lives so you can be free today. So either wait here for the punishment of the empire or leave this place."

A voice came from the crowd, "But where to?"

Roulan took over and replied, "You're free to do whatever you want. You can leave this place and start a new life, or you could join us. By us, I mean the two of us and four brave men. Not to mention a unique leader whose only dream in life is to take down the criminal Ceres. The choice is yours."

Nora raised her hand and concluded, "We're going to open this gate and leave for a better future. Whoever wants to live in the shadows, avoiding risks and danger shall not be welcomed, but those among you who seek dignity, glory, fight injustice, and leave their descendants with a legacy to tell in the next centuries, will be our brothers and sisters."

A loud screaming filled the area, and the two girls headed to the gates, leaving the castle. When they turned, an uncountable number of people followed behind.

CHAPTER 23

Alighieri dressed up as a merchant from the Union. His two friends, Arsalan and Sai had no choice but to play his slaves. This idea came to them after two days of thinking. They were aware of how dangerous their mission was, beginning with the supplies they needed, which were available only in markets close to the empire. Given that Arsalan and Sai were known in the Union, they had no room for error.

When Alighieri looked at the mirror, he admired himself and froze for a while. His golden hair went with the orange robe inlaid with pearls of different colors. He couldn't take his blue eyes off the mirror until a shadow appeared behind him. He turned and saw his two companions with frowning eyes.

The Solumy couldn't hold himself from laughing at their look, wearing dresses to the knees with no sleeves and faded brown sandals. They had picked a very particular market which most foreigners avoided for its reputation; the Lord of this market had eyes everywhere. Whenever he heard of wealthy foreign merchants in his Souk, he sent his soldiers pretending to be thieves ,to steal every valuable thing and took it to him.

Alighieri's clothes fooled people in the market. Some of them didn't delay informing the market owner, who was thrilled when they described the merchant to him, and immediately sent five of his best men to kill the slaves and rob Alighieri.

The robbers were used to this kind of mission and went for it enthusiastically, but instead of bringing gold and silver to their leader, they were offered a warm welcome ,then beaten until they couldn't stand on their feet.

Alighieri advanced to the shops and shouted, "This is a warning to everyone who considers himself smart enough to rob a man like me. The next who dares will be slaughtered like a goat, understood?" No one spoke, and Alighieri added, "I'm a wealthy man, willing to grow my business further. Behave yourselves and you shall make profits you had never dreamed of,"

The Solumy knew that his bluff would seduce the Souk's owner, remembering his father's saying, *"The greedy prevails over the liar."*

Alighieri's father wasn't wrong. The following day, one of the master's men came to them, waking them up with an invitation from the Souk's owner.

A huge table was expecting the three rebels, filled with chicken, beef, and four jars of juice with different flavors, not to mention the bread and all kinds of fruits.

Arsalan and Sai were delighted and filled their bellies, unlike Alighieri who was not interested in eating as much as making a deal with the Souk's owner. He sold them everything they needed at a reduced price, expecting that there would be bigger deals soon.

The following day, the three rebels took their ways, aiming for a secret place known only by their four friends. Sai was scared to death as they had to cross the forbidden forest, passing by at least seven barracks.

They were stopped in one barrack, and Alighieri's charm and generosity blinded the soldiers, they didn't have the slightest doubt that they were the wanted rebels.

Sai and Arsalan couldn't believe themselves when they crossed the forest safely. At night, they hunted a deer and shared it together.

While they were drinking a juice they purchased from the Souk, Arsalan asked Sai, "So, tell us what you learned from the Speakers!"

"Finally, someone apart from Ali and Roulan asks!" replied Sai and went to his bag. He fetched a giant orange egg and asked them what they thought it was.

"An ostrich eggs?" asked Alighieri.

"It has the same size, but it's not an egg, even though I called it an orange egg," replied Sai then threw it on the ground.

Both his friends stared at him, unable to follow. Then he asked Arsalan to hit the egg with one of his weapons. The Topraki hurled a dagger toward the orange egg and didn't miss. The clash left him and Alighieri petrified; a column of fire burst out, higher than anything they had ever seen.

Sai didn't stop there, and told them about other inventions, such as the grape arrows and the diggers. But his favorite one was the impenetrable wall, and he promised to demonstrate it the next day.

The following day, Sai kept his promise and decided to show them the impenetrable wall in action. He fetched two rectangular wooden molds from their supplies, put a large quantity of clay on each one, then poured water inside. After that, he picked up a little bag from his pocket filled with dark gray powder and poured it on one of the molds, then started kneading and adapting.

He waited until the bricks dried and planted them both in the soil.

Arsalan and Alighieri were just watching, they couldn't understand what he was up to. After that, Sai went to his horse to fetch two little black balls he called explosives. He placed each one next to the engraved bricks and asked his two friends to use their bows and shoot the little black balls.

Alighieri and Arsalan didn't question the command and did it. To their shock, one brick was destroyed and turned into wrecks, while the other one remained intact. Sai's companion both realized for the first time the meaning of the impenetrable wall.

***

Meanwhile, Ali and Keita went to the north. To Grond or what remained of it.

When Ceres built his empire and took over control, he decided to cleanse the kingdom because he didn't like the people who inhabited it and considered their black skin an error of the Creator. Ceres destroyed this kingdom, and those who survived his attacks, hid in the mountains until the emperor turned his attention to the other realms. They formed tribes and isolated themselves from the world.

It had been three days since Ali and Keita arrived. Four tribes refused to host them, thinking they were Union's spies.

Keita couldn't sleep at night, he bet that his people would accept Ali's offer.

The embarrassment killed him from the inside. As a result, some memories from his tragic life were raised. He remembered the first time he was taken away from his family and enslaved.

The tortures he suffered, and the lies he was told made him forget everything about his origins. The empire turned him into a killer, caring for one thing, the screaming of his fans in the Arena, when he took down his adversaries. He was spoiled by his owners and promised that one day he would be freed to join the army, which blinded him to feel any remorse when he took innocents' lives.

Finally, the day of his freedom came, and the only thing standing in his way was another fight. He was smart enough to know that his opponent won't be an ordinary one, so he hesitated to accept, thinking that he had to face the legendary gladiator, Ila.

He had never met Ila in person, but assumed he wouldn't stand against him, given what he had heard. Luckily his master told him Ila had left the Arena months ago, so he accepted the fight with no questions asked. He wasn't expecting someone easy, but he was wrong – it was an old black man with gray hair.

Keita's heart softened. He reached for his sword, but felt powerless and wondered, "How can I kill one of my own?" In the meantime, he remembered that one hit with his sword would bring him the freedom he'd been dreaming of, so he fetched his sword and approached his opponent.

The old man decided to drop his weapon and said, "What will you earn if you kill me?"

"My freedom," mumbled Keita.

The old man felt some innocence in his killer, so he decided to give him a piece of advice. "I'm a dead man, anyway. The last thing I expected was to be killed by one of my own people, but hear this from me, son, don't expect to be one of them one day. Remember, you were enslaved because of your color, so no matter what you do, you will always remain who you are."

The words from the old man were clumsy, but they touched Keita's heart and woke up some memories from his old life.

Everyone was expecting their gladiator to finish the Grondy old man. But Keita dropped his sword and said, "He lives," then walked away from the Arena's square, leaving everyone in the crowd shocked.

Empire of Rebels: Rise of Rebels

The coming days turned into hell for Keita. He had all sorts of torture, but luckily, it didn't last long, as one night, he slept in his cell and woke up in the forest unchained. All of his wounds were treated. He didn't know at the time that it was Ali's doing, the same man who was riding with him shoulder to shoulder.

Ali read his companion's mind and decided to release the heavy burden he carried, "There's always a light at the end of the tunnel. Don't worry, my friend, we'll figure it out."

Keita mumbled, "I wish I could make it easy for you this time!"

Ali smiled and said, "Remember, my friend, the harder things get, the bigger the reward. Plus, there are still other tribes, who knows?"

The sunset started when they were close to another tribe, so Ali suggested spending the night away from the tribe; it was common in all kingdoms that guests who arrived at night weren't always welcomed.

They slept and woke up when the sun rose. They had apples for breakfast and headed to the village. The drums started before they entered, and five guards stopped them at the entrance.

Keita spoke first, "Good day. My name is Keita, and this is my friend Ali. We want to speak with your leader."

The guard asked angrily, "And since when have the people of Turba been friends with us?"

Keita approached the guard and said through gritted teeth, "He's my guest!"

The guard's leader was intimidated by Keita's look and replied, "Fine, I'll check with our chief."

Keita and Ali didn't wait for long, and the soldier came back to them saying, "Our chief has agreed to meet with you, but you will have to hand over all of your weapons."

Keita looked at Ali, who nodded and did what they were told.

Keita wasn't very excited about this tribe. They were walking among tents in faded colors, the kids were playing around half-naked, and dirt was everywhere. They finally arrived at the leader's tent, which was different and bigger.

The chief was sitting with a smile on his face, raising his hand to the guard to leave them with him.

The man spoke acutely, "We call ourselves the Hawks. I'm their leader here. John is my name! And I welcome you on behalf of everyone."

The tow rebels agreed beforehand that Keita would do the talking since he was one of them, "Thank you, Lord John! My name is Keita, and this is my friend Ali. He's from Turba."

John looked at Ali, and a smile crossed his lips, "So you're the legendary knight who is making trouble for the empire."

Ali finally decided to speak, "I don't make trouble, my lord. I'm only claiming what was once ours."

Keita interrupted to avoid the first disagreement, "Lord John, we came here to seek your help. We want to build a refuge for oppressed men and women."

As expected, the reaction of John was not different from the other leaders. The only difference with the Hawks' leader, was that he had some courtesy to explain it. "Having you here will draw the empire's attention. I accepted to meet you out of courtesy, because I admire what this great man Ali is doing. But the Empire's eyes are everywhere. They have weapons that can bring down any castle, their number is growing, and they can swallow all our tribes in half a day. I'm sorry. I wish I could help you, but I only care about keeping my people alive. Bringing you here will draw their attention, and I can't let that happen."

Keita and Ali spent hours explaining their plan and its efficiency, but John kept his answer the same. "No."

Keita was furious, but he kept his rage to himself and begged his friend to not stay another hour in the village. Ali agreed.

They took their weapons from the guards and left. Ali was pretending to be optimistic, but deep down, he was disappointed. At sunset, they stopped to camp in the woods, and while they were trying to set a fire, they heard footsteps.

Ali reached for his sword, and Keita placed an arrow in his bow. They both lowered their weapons when they saw who it was. A woman in her fifties with two unarmed young men. She handed a white bag to Ali and told him, "We brought you something to eat."

Ali took the bag and replied, "Thank you, my lady! Grondies are known for their generosity. Still, I'd dare to ask who you are? And why did you trouble yourselves to bring us food?"

"My name is Nadufa, and I'm John's sister. This is my son Mamadou and his cousin Jibril; John's son."

The two young men approached Ali and knelt. Then Jibril said, "We heard about what you did to the empire, and it's an honor to finally meet you, my lord."

Ali exchanged a look of confusion with Keita, and Nadufa added, "These young men, along with others, are going on your path. They started hunting the empire's soldiers months ago."

Ali was delighted, hope was rising even in the destroyed kingdom, so he said, "Jibril, Mamadou, stand up. Never kneel before any man. It's a delight to see young men like you seeking justice."

Mamadou had tears in his eyes, when he heard Ali stating his name, so he replied enthusiastically, "Consider us your servants along with another seventy-one courageous men and women. We choose your path. Either we take down the empire, or we die trying."

Nadufa added, "I overheard you earlier with my brother. I assure you that he's no coward. The death of our brother devastated him. I have a piece of land that might be suitable for your project."

Ali smiled and, in a reassuring tone said, "We have a man called Sai. His mind can beat the winter."

The day after, Ali sent messages to his other five friends and surprised Keita by saying, "You're in charge now, until Alighieri arrives."

Keita, in shock, replied, "What about you?"

"I need to consult the Thinkers about something."

Chapter 24

Ceres was living his worst days, starting with his health, which wasn't doing well; he could hardly sleep at night. His daughter had betrayed him and had no love left for him, and the rebels' power kept growing.

For the first time in his entire life, he felt defeated. Still, he was a pragmatic ruler leaving no door open for sorrows. He mobilized every power in his empire and didn't care about what Roulan and Nora did in Dharatee.

The emperor knew it would keep happening as long as Ali was alive, so his attention turned to this man, and assigned his most trustable advisor Ramessess to bring Ali's head.

Ceres was sitting in his council waiting for the prime advisor and the military chief, who didn't delay joining him.

Ceres addressed the military chief first, "Any news about the princess?"

"Everything is under control, your highness. No one got in her chamber or out, except for her servants and Sofia, her friend."

Ceres replied, "She's a troublemaker, don't underestimate her."

"I won't, your highness. We sealed all the windows, and there are guards all over the place," replied Vlad, then Ceres thanked and dismissed him.

Ceres turned to Ramessess and spoke with a tone full of sorrow, "Lord Ramessess, I can see delight in your eyes. Anything you want to share?"

"Indeed, your highness. I have great news," replied Ramessess,

Ceres' face didn't change. To him, there was nothing that could make him feel better except Ali's head. So he yelled, "I don't see Ali's head in your hand!"

Ramessess smiled, "What if I tell you that I will bring it to you in less than three days?"

The prime advisor finally got the emperor's attention, who stood and asked Ramessess, "Keep talking!"

Ramessess did so with enthusiasm. "As you know, my lord, our eyes are everywhere. Ali was spotted three days ago in the tribes of the north. He went to their leaders to seek refuge for his companions, but no one granted him his wish. The news was very tough on him, so he got separated from his band and headed to the west. There's no kingdom in that direction. The only place he would seek in these circumstances is the Blessing Tree."

Ceres' wasn't very excited and replied, "This is just an assumption, Ramessess. He might be leading us to a trap!"

"I have considered that, your highness, i already sent three men to spy on him," answered Ramessess,

When finally Ceres' face started changing, he added, "I'm going to lead the attack myself."

Ceres somehow felt relieved; he knew there was only one man who could bring this rebel. Without a doubt, was his prime advisor.

***

Ali had no idea about the trap he was walking to. He felt hopeful again, as his plan was going exactly as he had designed it with his companions. They knew if somehow a shred of their plan reached the ears of the emperor or Ramessess, everything would go in vain and undergo the same consequences as the initial one.

Ali read a lot of history and knew that secrets tended to expose themselves, so he relied on speeding up the process, using one of his last pigeons and sending it to his friends inviting them to come to the new land. Sadly, he couldn't stay with Keita and the new rebels.

Instead, he decided to go to the Thinkers, which was necessary for his plan to work. He remembered the last time when he didn't follow their advice. His act of rescuing King Eleah cost him four thousand people, as well as Isaac, so their blessing was a must.

On his way to the blessing tree, he started picturing his future. He had no desire to rule or collect wealth. All he wanted was to take down the empire and have a normal life with a wife, many sons and daughters. A few months before, Ali had one ambition: destroying Ceres and restoring the world to its state before the Union.

His mind had never thought about anything until his eyes met his enemy's daughter, Leah, the girl who shook every inch of his body. From then, he had added to his wish list the prospect of growing older with a woman. At the same time, given the circumstances, he knew how hard it was. He thought they would never end up together, although he was persuaded by that thought, he still enjoyed thinking about her and building an imaginary world where she could fit.

Less than a mile before he arrived, he started feeling danger around him. He heard and saw nothing, but his gut kept telling him he wasn't alone, and he was right.

The next thing he saw was two arrows hitting his horse in the neck.

Ali tumbled from his mount and quickly regained his footing, unsheathing his sword as he prepared to face his attackers. The figures of Union soldiers began to emerge from every direction, their numbers quickly surpassing ten.

The leader of the group removed his helmet, revealing himself as Ramessess, the second man on Ali's list of the most despised enemies. He laughed mockingly. "It seems your friends have abandoned you. Why don't you just drop your weapon and surrender? The emperor is eager to see you."

Ali hid his fear and replied with a sneer, "Why didn't the emperor come himself instead of sending his lapdogs?"

Ramessess' expression turned dark as he barked out the command, "Drop your weapon!"

"Come and take it!" Ali shot back in a rage, throwing his dagger at Ramessess, who narrowly dodged it, instead it found the chest of one of his soldiers. Ramessess screamed, "Seize him! I want him alive!"

A soldier shot an arrow at Ali, who blocked it with his sword. Ramessess shouted, "Idiot! I said I want him alive!"

Three soldiers advanced on Ali at once, but he ran towards them with his sword, kicking one and using it to block the second and pierce his belly. He then kneeled to avoid the third soldier's attack and cut off his right foot. The first soldier tried to stand, but Ali's sword found his throat.

Ali was moving quickly among the soldiers, avoiding their hits and taking them down one by one. Ramessess couldn't stand it any longer and shot an arrow at Ali's shoulder, but he didn't let go of his sword and kept fighting. Another arrow hit his thigh, and a third hit his arm. Ali's strength was weakening, and a soldier finally pierced him with a spear in his back.

He fell to the ground, and Ramessess screamed, "Stupid soldiers! I said I need him alive!"

But it was too late, and Ramessess' plan for Ali's capture had failed. He ordered one of his remaining soldiers to cut off Ali's head. The soldier eagerly complied, but before the blade could touch Ali's throat, an arrow pierced the soldier's hand, and another found his neck.

Empire of Rebels: Rise of Rebels

A masked figure emerged, throwing down his bow and charging towards the remaining soldiers, leaving Ramessess to flee in terror.

Ali was delighted to see one of his friends had finally arrived, even though he thought he was dying. At least he would receive a proper burial. The masked figure kneeled beside him and removed his mask, revealing the most beautiful face Ali had ever seen: Leah. Her blue eyes were filled with tears as she spoke in a firm voice, "Don't say anything. I'm going to save you."

She broke the arrows and examined his wounds, the amount of blood beneath him indicating a deep injury. She tore a piece of fabric from his tunic and pressed it to the wound to stop the bleeding.

Ali coughed twice and spoke in a low voice, "Why did you come to my rescue?"

Leah held her tears and decided to face reality, thinking that the man was throwing his last breaths. She pulled herself together and chose to give him beautiful words before he left her world. "I don't know, but I couldn't let a man like you die."

Ali smiled, coughing twice. "I can't ask for more; hearing this made me realize I have lived everything beautiful in this world," then turned his head left and said nothing.

Leah couldn't hold herself and kept shouting his name, "Ali!"

***

Ramessess was galloping to the Union, scared to be followed by this knight who was like a devil. The prime advisor also started thinking about what he would tell his emperor. The mission didn't go as planned, but the outcome was good.

It would have been better if he returned with Ali's head, but in his mind, there was no way that the Turban could survive the spear and all the arrows. To reassure Ceres, he chose to add some lies, and that's what he did when he entered the council. He saw the look of Ceres, who didn't wait until his prime advisor knelt, "You said you're going to bring the rebel's head, so where is it?"

"Ali is dead, my lord. He cost me all the soldiers. I shot him with three arrows, and a spear pierced his back. I saw him dying. While I was going to cut his head and bring it to you, other rebels surprised us and we were outnumbered, so I chose to run."

Given Ceres' character, he wouldn't be certain without seeing the body. But he forced himself to believe Ali was dead, screaming and praising Ramessess, who asked enthusiastically, "What's next, your highness?"

"The snake has lost its head. We're going to take care of the other rebels and those who followed them," replied Ceres and didn't stop, "But now, we're going to celebrate!"

Chapter 25

Ali's companions finally got together in the north of Grond, a land with a very tough winter. In addition to the cold weather, darkness dominated the whole day, giving the sun a few hours to rise and set. Nadufa informed them that winter would start in two months, so they had no choice but to begin .

Sai didn't have a chance to get enough of his wife and got to his work right away. He was aware of how crucial his role was. Luckily, he had enough young men and women to get to work and selected eighty among them. Thirty were assigned a critical task, which was making the resisting powder; a gray substance that makes walls unbreachable.

The task required meticulous hands, so all of them were girls. The other fifty brought the clay to one place to ease the task for the remaining workers, to knead it and make it in molds. Everyone got involved , as they had to make ten thousand bricks in a day.

Arsalan was putting a lot of pressure on the blacksmiths to make long iron tubes. They succeeded on the third day, and the building process started. The atmosphere was jovial. Most of them were singing.

The plan was to build a wall of forty feet height, so Sai instructed them to make blocks ten feet in height and ten in width. Then they attached each four together with nails and a special glue. In the meantime, another team's role was to dig twelve feet deep, so the blocks could be placed there using cords.

It took them two weeks to finish a rectangular building, huge enough to hold all their three thousand people. Another team was inside, building houses to protect them from the winter. They placed iron tubes horizontally between bricks. Sai's idea was to fill these tubes with hot water, so they could warm these walls in the winter. Sai's team remained outside, strengthening the walls more and more.

The new mastermind was working on one last project with Alighieri and five members of his team; they were digging together a well at the back of the wall. No one was aware of this except them and Ali, who suggested it in the first place. The other five rebels were with Nadufa, designing the plan of defense.

Nora couldn't hide her anxiety, as Ali should have returned two days ago. Her friends kept reassuring her he is fine, but deep down, she knew they were wrong.

A moment later, Sai entered with Jibril and Mamadu. Roulan had never seen these two young men in her life, so she advanced and asked Sai who they were. Keita intervened with a smile and said,

"These are two courageous men, Jibril and Mamadu, and they were causing a lot of trouble to the Union before we came."

The two young men didn't exchange smiles with Keita. On the contrary, their faces were pale. Keita noticed and asked firmly, "What's wrong?"

They didn't reply. Arsalan couldn't stand the silence and the look on these two young men, and yelled, "What's wrong, Keita?"

"I sent them behind Ali," replied Keita.

Arsalan went immediately to Mamadu, holding him by the neck. "What's wrong, boy? Why do you look troubled?"

Mamadu couldn't reply and started crying, Jibril held Arsalan's hand and spoke in a whined tone, "We arrived too late."

Then he fetched from inside his robe Ali's sword.

Arsalan released Mamadu and grasped the sword, checked it, and said, "A knight like Ali loses his sword only if…" he couldn't complete his sentence.

Nadufa spoke to her nephew, "Jibril, tell us what happened!"

"We arrived at the Blessing Tree. There were bodies of the Union's soldiers all over the place. We found Ali's sword there. Still, we had hope he made it alive, so we went to the empire's castle, and there was a celebration inside. A woman told us that the occasion was the death of Ali."

Roulan fell on her knees, unable to scream or say anything. Sai went next to a wall, started punching it, and ignored the pain and blood on his knuckles.

Keita's face became wet with tears dropping heavily and screaming. As for Arsalan he could neither speak nor move in total shock. Even Alighieri had his eyes full of tears, but he pulled himself together, asking Jibril if they saw his body.

"His head was hung on the wall!" replied Jibril.

The screaming went higher. Nadufa was trying to calm them down, but she couldn't. Alighieri was drowning in his sorrows, but remembered his friend Ali who always asked him to keep an eye on the group because, without them, the cause would go in vain. So he yelled three times to get their attention. He wiped his tears and started, "My friends, this is a tragedy that affects the whole world. The earth, with its trees and mountains, will cry eternally for losing such a man. But he's a mortal like any of us. There's no time for people like us to grieve. Remember, you all took an oath to his cause, so either we honor him by following his path or leave the world in the hands of those who killed him."

Nora did nothing except stare at them, then walked toward Jibril and Mamadou. "Was it his head hanging on the wall, or someone else's?"

"We couldn't tell, my lady, it was too far away. But everybody was talking about his death in the castle." replied Jibril.

"Then it's just one of Ceres' games. Ali isn't dead."

No one replied, and she realized they were thinking she was a fool.

"Wake up people. This is Ali we're talking about! He cannot die."

Still, no one dared to contradict her. She raised her tone, "What kind of weapon can kill Ali? A spear? It can never pierce his body. A sword? It will break before touching his skin. An Arrow? It will change its direction to not touch him. Ali is the hope for the whole world and I refuse to accept he is dead. He will join us and lead us in our war against Ceres."

Nora went next to Arsalan and asked him to hand her his sword, and he did it without resisting. Then she left them.

Nadufa spoke again, "It is a tragedy, and none of us could replace Ali, but he'd been working on this for a decade. We need to carry on his work, whether we succeed or not!". No reaction came from the five rebels, so she carried on, "There's no shame in crying your friend, do that tonight, but remember, we have more than three thousand people to whom we made many promises!"

She then left them there crying for their friend, Ali, and they weren't the only ones to cry for him.

***

Three days ago, Leah was next to Ali, when he was throwing his last breaths. She was screaming and doing her best to save him, but she couldn't. He was in front of her, not moving.

Leah had suffered her entire life from loneliness and sadness, her mother left a hole in her heart, and the princess never expected, that one day it would be healed until the rebel showed up in her life.

Her heart had beaten abnormally the first time she saw him, thinking his charm and manliness made her feel that way, but she was wrong. Instead, his devotion to his cause, his loyalty to his friends, and how he cared about the weakest people made her admire him.

She felt sad to see a man like Ali with such devotion died by the hands of an evil man like Ramessess.

Suddenly, she heard footsteps from behind. Leah retrieved her dagger, turning with an angry look and a willing to kill whoever showed up. But she lowered her weapon, when she saw who he was; a bald man with a few gray hairs. He looked to be in his sixties, she knew from his white robe he was a Speaker. Her anger made her forget her manners and spoke with him harshly: "What do you want?"

The man didn't reply. He approached and knelt towards Ali. He placed his index under the rebel's nose and shouted, "He's still breathing, but hardly," and then turned Ali to his right side to inspect his wounds. He looked closely and turned him back.

After that, he put some slight pressure on the belly and explained,

"His kidney and liver weren't touched. Help me take off his shirt."

Leah was in shock, but she obeyed the old man blindly. She took her dagger and cut off Ali's leather top.

The old man used a liquid, that he fetched from his bag and poured it on the wound in Ali's back. He started cleaning it with a white cloth, then took an ointment and spread it all over the wound, and used a bandage to cover it. He did the same thing to the other three injuries.

"We can't leave him here. The cold in the open air makes his state more critical. Let's take him next to the Blessing Tree." Then he handed Leah some medicines and instructed her how to take care of the wounds.

Leah understood nothing and shouted, "You're not going anywhere. You should take care of him!"

"He's under your care. You're the one who saved his life," replied the Speaker.

Leah argued, "But I don't know how? Please stay with us!"

The Speaker smiled and replied, "Don't worry, Princess Leah. You've been here before – do your usual rituals, and a higher power will guide you! Farewell!"

She remembered what Rio had told her; holding his hand and thinking of happy memories.

After a few hours, she woke up in a familiar cave. Ali was next to her, and she could hear his breathing. Joy filled her heart, and although she wished she could wake him up, she preferred not to. He needed time to relax.

While she was cleaning his face from the blood, a voice filled the area, "You choose wisely. Your destiny is as great as his!"

Leah said nothing, and the voice asked her why she killed her people to save him.

Leah didn't know what to say in the beginning, then decided to speak her heart. "They're bad people who deserved to die, but I don't know if I did this to fight evil, or because I was selfish, and all I cared about was to save the man I'm in love with."

"If only all people followed their hearts and minds like you did!" replied the voice, and silence dominated the place.

A sound of coughing pricked her ears, and she went quickly to Ali, who was moving his head. Leah grabbed a bottle of water, raised his head gently, and helped him drink.

Ali drank two sips and opened his eyes slowly to see the most beautiful pair of eyes. She smiled and said, "You're not dead."

Ali found his voice, and smiled, "Does it matter?"

Leah chuckled softly and kept taking care of him for over three days. His wounds were healing abnormally fast, and unlike Leah, Ali wasn't surprised. He explained that the cave was a holy place which can make miracles."

CHAPTER 26

Ceres continued the celebration for a whole week, thinking his enemy Ali was gone. It made him so ecstatic, he forgot all about his health issues. As for his daughter, he knew that time would bring her back.

Ramessess' spies kept bringing information about the rebels' work, but the emperor wasn't worried at all. On the contrary, the fact that they got together in one place, would ease the task of eliminating them all. His military chief Vlad had already started the army preparation, and to their advantage, one of Ramessess' spies infiltrated the rebels' building, and fed Vlad with valuable intelligence; the walls, the number of soldiers, and some of their tactics. The spy was close to Jibril and Mamadu, who naively shared everything they knew with him.

The only thing he missed was the powder Sai had made, because Alighieri kept its effect confidential between him, Arsalan, and Sai. Even Keita and the girls weren't aware of it.

The emperor convened all the generals to his council, so they could discuss the new strategy to deal with Ali's companions. The appearance of these rebels cost Ceres a lot: for starters his daughter – who hadn't spoken to him for more than a week, hundreds of soldiers, and on top of that, two generals, Philip and Peter. The emperor knew that without changing his current politics, other rebels would show up shortly. But for the time being, he preferred to deal with the existing rebels and shut down their flame. With no introduction, he asked Vlad about his plan of attack.

The military chief held his mustache and boasted, "My spy advised they have an army of three thousand people. Some are well-trained soldiers, and others are just commoners. They have built a wall of forty feet in height, which surrounds houses they built."

The new treasury chief, William, was the first to comment. "You said they're three thousand people who aren't all soldiers, yet I heard you're taking twenty thousand soldiers. Isn't that a lot?"

Vlad didn't seem pleased by such a question, and William added, "Forgive me, Lord Vlad, I'm no military man. I just look at things from a financial perspective. It's a long way to the north. The supplies and the food this army would need is a fortune, not to mention the wages of soldiers and compensations the martyrs' families would demand."

Vlad was offended and swore to himself that William would pay, but in the presence of the emperor and Ramessess, he decided to be diplomatic. "No apology needed, Lord William. We both care about the interest of the empire. There are tribes all over the north. If they all decided to join the rebels, we'd be dealing with more than ten thousand. It's very unlikely to happen, but I prefer to consider the odds. A victory is more important than gold."

Ceres supported the decision of Vlad, and so did Ramessess and the rest of the generals.

They carried on the discussion, covering what would happen after vanquishing the rebels' army.

When they were done, Ceres called his personal guard Eliot and asked him to bring his daughter Leah to the council.

Eliot mumbled, "Your highness, what if she refuses as usual!"

"Use force, if necessary!"

Eliot expressed his fear again, "Your highness, she will break my neck if I do."

Ceres stood and yelled, "Then you have no use in my castle! Do what you were asked!"

Eliot couldn't disobey the emperor and went straight to her chamber. He informed her, she immediately went to the council and found her father sitting on his chair with a face completely different from the last time. It was full of joy. She knelt, "Your highness".

He walked towards her, held her by the shoulders, and said, "Since when I'm not your father."

"I'm sorry, father. My behavior last time was disobedient. I don't deserve to be your daughter," she couldn't hold herself back from crying.

Ceres held her chin gently to raise her head and replied, "You'll always be my daughter. I don't mind you speaking your mind, when you're unhappy with my decisions. You're a valuable advisor to me, as much as Ramessess."

"No father. Only men do such things. I prefer to step out from politics and find a suitable husband, with whom I can give you many grandsons," replied Leah.

Ceres was relieved to hear his daughter's decision, and informed her, she could do whatever suited her, as long as she stayed next to him.

But Ceres didn't know that his daughter teamed up with her friend Sofia, since she had been locked in her chamber. Apart from the servants, Sofia was the only person allowed to access her room. She brought her all the news from the council. That was mainly thanks to Eliot, who was so insanely in love with Sofia that he spilled all the council's secrets. When he found out about how the girls had used him, he didn't mind because, in addition to his feelings for the princess' friend, he owed his life to Ali who had spared him once.

Leah could trust her friends Sofia and Eliot ,as they had both helped her before. One day, she discovered the plan to trap Ali.

Upon hearing about Ramessess' plan for Ali, Leah decided to escape her imprisonment. Sofia and Leah fooled all the guards by taking advantage of their similar height.

Sofia pretended to be visiting Leah in her chamber. Then Leah took her friend's clothes and left the room, making everyone believe she was Peter's daughter.

Eliot was expecting Leah in the stable and helped her to sneak out of the castle. She had been lucky to arrive before Ali's execution, so she could save his life and make it back to the castle using the same strategy. It worked.

The princess decided not to stop there and kept relying on Eliot, to bring her valuable information from the council, so she could send it to Ali.

***

Ali was close to his new home in the north. He was confident that Alighieri and the rest of the team would carry on with the agreed-upon plan.

He was partially correct. They all got over their grieving, except for Nora and Keita. They had lost their determination and couldn't be as helpful as before.

Alighieri convened the whole team to discuss what was coming. They had no idea when the Union will attack, but they were sure it would be sometimes soon. And while discussing every excruciating detail, they heard the drums banging. Roulan stopped talking and said, "Is that the empire's army?"

Arsalan, with a scared tone, replied, "What else could it be?"

Before they moved, one of the Dharatians knocked on the door and came in when he was granted, "My lords, there's a knight next to the gate. He said he was a friend!"

Alighieri smiled and said, "He must be the reinforcement."

The six rebels and Nadufa left their small chamber to welcome the knight. He was standing in the square when the gate was opened. It was still far to recognize who he was, but not for Roulan; she ran to her husband and grabbed him by his shoulder. The tears overcame her, making her voice break, "Am I dreaming?"

Sai replied, "If it's a dream, I prefer not to wake up."

The picture got more apparent, and the screaming filled the area. It was Ali in the flesh, advancing slowly with his horse. Keita couldn't wait any longer and ran towards him. Ali got off his horse and hugged his friend. The others joined. Ali felt an additional dose of life fill in his heart. Seeing what his friends had done in less than a month left him agape.

Then he noticed the absence of his Token friend and asked about her with a worried tone. Before anyone answered, he saw her walking in his direction with a sword in her hand.

She came closer and handed him his sword, "I never believed you were dead."

Ali kept smiling, and Arsalan added, "Unlike Nora, we thought you were dead!"

"So did I, my friend, but somehow I survived. I guess you're still stuck with me!"

Ali stared at the walls and, in an admiring tone, said, "It's amazing what you've done, my friends. All of this in less than two months."

Ali was looking at the huge wall, the brown houses, and the long tower. He tried to speak many times, but the words couldn't come out, leaving him amazed.

Alighieri invited them all into a small chamber with a rectangular table. There were five chairs on each side, one in the front. Alighieri went to the right side next to Keita and Arsalan. Nadufa and the girls sat in front of them.

"After you, Lord Ali," said Alighieri, pointing to the seat in the front.

Ali thanked them and sat, then immediately delivered scary news. They all were shocked when they heard the number of soldiers Ceres will send. They thought it would be ten thousand at most, but when Ali informed them that the number is twice what they were expecting, they were terrified.

Ali agreed with them, considering the rebel forces were around three thousand, half of them had never carried a weapon. And although they had started intensive training, they couldn't be compared to soldiers who spent their entire lives in the military.

Nadufa stood and suggested, "We still have time. I mean, we can send for reinforcement from the other tribes."

"Isn't that what you were trying to do in the last five years?" asked Alighieri

Nadufa looked at Alighieri, then at Ali. "Yes, they said no, because we seemed weak. But now with these walls and you folks, we have a shot. Plus we have nothing to lose. With your permission Ali, I can send my son Mamadu for this mission."

Ali looked at his friends. From their eyes, he understood they were on board and granted what Nadufa suggested.

Before going to sleep, Ali delivered another piece of bad news, "I have eyes in the emperor's castle, who continuously delivers me good information, and I heard they have a spy here."

It shocked everyone, Ali added, "Let's keep our eyes open. Everything we say here in this council can't leave the seven of us."

With this heavy news, they went to sleep. Arsalan checked that the guards were all in their positions and returned to the dormitory.

The walls were guarded by thirty men. Jibril was one of them, he was a man who preferred not to talk a lot, isolating himself in a corner and staring at the sky. He loved counting the stars and giving each one of them a name.

That night the cloud covered everything, and instead, he was contemplating what Sai had managed to do in less than two months.

Suddenly Jibril glimpsed a shadow inside the tower. It seemed very strange, because the only people allowed in that place were Ali and Sai. He decided to inspect the area, so he called one of the guards and asked him to watch for him, then sneaked to the tower.

Jibril realized he was right. He recognized the man inside – he was Dharatian. Jibril kept a low profile and suddenly saw the man carrying a pigeon.

John's son decided to leave the tower, and went down with his eyes on the windows. The minute the pigeon came out, he shot it with an arrow, and the poor bird fell. Jibri had assumed right, he found a letter attached to its leg, and without hesitation, he took it and ran to his position.

By the time he made it there, the Dharatian spy came at him and cut his back twice. He started searching Jibril's pocket for the letter and fortunately one of the guards saw what was happening. He screamed, "Murdered, Murderer…"

Another guard rang the giant bell. The spy was cornered, and in a matter of seconds, ten soldiers surrounded him.

Ali ran toward Jibril whose mouth was bleeding. He forced a smile, "I wish I could fight next to you, my lord."

Ali tore a piece of his shirt and placed it on the wound, "Don't talk my friend, help on its way. You'll fight next to me."

These were the last words Jibril heard.

Nadufa joined her nephew too late. Ali turned to her and lowered his head. She didn't scream, and neither could she hold her tears. Then she closed her nephew's eyes and whispered a few prayers in his ears.

One guard came to Ali, handed him a piece of paper, and said, "We found who did this. He stole this from Jibril."

Ali took the letter and read it loudly. "Ali is alive."

Then threw the letter and asked Nadufa, "How do you want to handle this?"

"You deal with the traitor who killed Jibril. I'll ride to my brother to inform him myself," replied Nadufa.

Ali and his companions couldn't sleep the whole night. Although the spy was exposed and imprisoned, a great promising knight had lost his life. In addition to the sorrows and regrets, Ali was also expecting a reaction from Jibril's father – a leader of a tribe with more than two thousand soldiers.

If he took the news badly, and held Ali responsible for the death of his son, there wouldn't have been anyone left to fight the Union. Still, Ali continued with his plan. He assigned Roulan to extract information from the spy and waited for the sun to rise, so he could speak to his people about the death of Jibril.

Everyone gathered in the square between the houses and the wall. Ali was already standing with his six companions.

"People of Grond and Dharatee, today our friend Jibril lost his life trying to protect us from treason. We're all sad about the loss of this man. This is war, and there are always people who pay with their lives, which is a huge loss for us. But not for Jibril. After all, we'll all die, but how many would die defending their beloved ones?

"As for the traitor who killed him, I don't consider him a Dharatian, because to earn the right to be part of the great seven kingdoms, you need to be decent and honorable, like those who founded these realms. We're working night and day to ensure our people's safety, don't let this tragedy distract you. Remember why you're here."

Alighieri shouted, "For a better world without the empire!"

The others followed with the exact words, and kept repeating them until the drums started banging.

The gate was opened, and Nadufa showed up with her brother, Jibril's father.

His face was mixed with sadness and anger. Ali didn't wait and advanced. He stopped and put his hand on his heart, "Please accept my condolences. Jibril was under our protection, and he was murdered. I take full responsibility for it. You can take my life if you see me as equal to your son. All I ask is to avoid war between us, especially now."

John looked at Ali, then slowly turned his eyes, looking around, "Jibril was an extraordinary boy. He always wanted to restore the glory of his grandfathers, but he was missing the ways to do it, until you showed up in his life. You guided him and offered him the happiness he was lacking since his mother died."

Ali was reassured that there would be no conflicts. He kept reminding John that he was the one who instilled courage and great values in him, but John knew that Ali was trying to be nice, so he chose not to disagree with him further. Instead, he mumbled,

"With your permission, I want to bury my son next to his mother."

Ali agreed with no questions asked. Sai had already made a wooden coffin. They cleaned Jibril and made him wear white clothes in line with the traditions of Grondies. After that, John took his son and left the castle.

Roulan couldn't extract any additional information from the spy, and Ali decided to execute him in front of everyone to set an example. He did it on purpose to have a Grondy execute him, so they won't place any blame on their new allies, the Dharatians.

Nadufa volunteered to execute the spy, thinking it would calm her rage. The murderer was brought by two of her men.

Roulan hit behind his knee to have him kneel, the detainee couldn't disobey Nadufa when she told him, "Lower your head!"

Jibril's aunt raised her hand, and aimed with all of her strength at the back of his neck. One hit was enough to make his head roll over next to her feet.

Chapter 27

Ali woke up to Sai's voice shouting that a homing pigeon had landed on the wall. Without even changing, Ali ran outside and climbed the stairs. The bird came immediately to him, and the rebels' leader fetched the letter to read it. When he looked downstairs, his six companions were already standing with sleepy faces. He shouted, "It's a message from our friend in the Union. Twenty thousand soldiers are coming, they'll be here in three days. You know what to do!"

Indeed, everyone knew what to do precisely. The tactic was to split their three thousand soldiers into four teams.

One of them was the archers, led by Nora and Roulan. This team had spent the last two months training intensively on shooting.

They would be on top of the wall, and were trained to do two things: shoot without missing and obey Nora and Roulan to the letter. The old people refused to stand without participating. Nora found them a valuable role, which was to prepare the arrows for the shooters during the attack. The task seemed useless to most people, but Nora's idea was to speed up the shooting.

A third team was about a thousand soldiers led by Arsalan and Keita. This team will be hiding behind a hill ,which is about half a mile away from the walls. They were instructed to stay still and not move toward the enemy ,unless they received two arrows in their direction. If it was only one, it would be a sign to join the wall. The shooting was going to be done by Nora

The fourth team would be staying inside the castle. Ali and Alighieri remained with them. This team didn't have an exact plan. Ali and his friend will improvise depending on the outcome of Roulan and Nora's team.

As for Sai, he was preparing a big surprise for the enemy, which he called the Show. He only revealed the result to Ali, Roulan, and his team. He went outside the wall, about three hundred feet away. He was accompanied by the thirty women, who helped make the resisting powder.

Sai instructed them to plant the orange eggs. They placed more than seven hundred along the width of the walls.

Ali didn't ignore the power of communication with Keita, and assigned three men to do that. One was on the wall bringing the information from the Turban leader, and two were outside taking information to the army behind the hill.

When Ali learned that the enemy was approaching, he gathered the soldiers inside the building and made

Empire of Rebels: Rise of Rebels

one last speech, "How often has a small host overcome a great host? Only when its people realize that it was never about who had a bigger number, rather the ones whose hearts were filled with good. Do you see this woman?" Ali pointed at Roulan, "With her husband, they killed 147 soldiers from the enemy without even a knife."

He then raised his tone, "Remember you're doing this for you and your descendants. We have many surprises for the enemy, and I promise you a victory. If you make it out alive, you will enjoy a life with dignity and honor." Ali stopped, "And wealth, obviously."

A burst of laughter filled the square, then Ali shouted, "And those who lose their lives, their descendants will walk with their names like a crown on their heads. Their bravery will mark history for hundreds of years ."

Alighieri chanted, "For a better life!"

"From now on, our name is the Free People," concluded Ali.

More news spread motivation, when Mamadu entered the wall with five hundred extra soldiers, thirsty for the Unionist's blood. Ali ordered them to join Arsalan and Keita.

Everyone went to their positions when darkness fell. Their hearts started pumping as they waited for the enemy to show up any minute.

The scary view on the horizon shook the hearts of everyone on Roulan and Nora's team. With every soldier from the enemy carrying a torch, it looked like a cloud of fire moving to burn the Free People. Ali was there too. Roulan looked at him, and he nodded, giving her permission to speak to her team, "Don't be scared. Remember we're the ones behind the wall, and we're all great shooters."

The army finally arrived and stopped six hundred feet away. They ranked all along the width of the wall.

Twenty catapults were rolling out of the ranks. Ali and Sai had expected that, but another thing confused them.

Big rectangular boxes with wheels were being pushed by four soldiers each. Sai had never seen or read about anything like it.

Ali noticed Sai's scared face, and asked him not to give much thought to it.

The enemy expected the archers to start shooting, but they were instructed not to. Instead, they hid behind the wall.

The Union leader raised his hand to start firing the catapults. And just like that, it began.

A ball the size of a wagon launched like an arrow toward the wall. Twenty of these balls were thrown all at the same time, followed by two similar batches. The sound of the clash was like thunder.

The Union's leader was smiling proudly, expecting the wall to fall, but when the dust was gone, the wall remained intact.

Nora and Roulan gave the signals, and their team started showing up at the top of the wall. The Token girl yelled, "Archers to the shooting line!"

Two hundred shooters placed their arrows in their bows and were ready to shoot.

The Union soldiers prepared their shields against the enemy's. The Unionist leader was behind, observing what was happening, and his eye caught something strange.

The archers were directing their arrows downward and not upward. At such a distance, it was impossible for any arrow to reach even the first line of his army, and he knew they couldn't be that dumb given the reputation of their leaders, who were fierce warriors.

While he was trying to decipher this trickery, the first shot was made, and his assumption was correct.

The archers weren't aiming for the heads of the Union's men, but instead for the small orange balls that Sai and his team planted. When every arrow touched the little ball, a flame burst from the land like a tree trunk and stretched higher than the walls.

The arrows kept coming down, and the soldiers of the Union were stuck in their place, unable to believe what they were seeing. Soon, seven hundred flames higher than any tree formed the shape of a giant prison door.

Sai advised that the fire wouldn't stay for long, so Roulan echoed the same command as Nora did before, "Archers to the shooting line!"

Roulan gave the signal and five hundred arrows were released at once toward the Union's army. They placed their shields in front and above them, expecting the shafts to hit the iron shields and fall, but they weren't regular arrows. Their heads had a small gray ball instead of a pointy end, when it hit anything, it exploded. The Union's soldiers were terrorized from seeing the blood and intestines of their friends flying above their heads.

The remains of the fire lit up what was happening there, thousands of soldiers were down.

Nora was smiling proudly, tasting the victory. She spoke with Ali, who was not so far from her, "Shall I send the signal to Arsalan and Keita?"

Ali wasn't as excited as her. His only answer was, "Not yet."

The big rectangular boxes Ali saw earlier worried him. The Union's soldiers were pulling them in the front, and there were no more grape arrows to destroy them – only the regular ones that hit the Unionist shields and fell.

The enemy revealed their secret weapon by untying each rectangular box's cords.

There were at least twenty collapsed ladders against each other. When released, the box expanded, and each ladder went in front of the other, forming long diagonal ladders.

The front of it had hooks stuck at the walls from the inside. The Unionists started climbing and covering themselves with special shields that protected their front and head.

The front shields had two holes, allowing the soldiers to keep an excellent visual. The rebels' arrows couldn't touch them, and hundreds were climbing ladders towards the wall, using their crossbows to shoot, which unlike the regular bow, each one could load up to five arrows.

The Free People started falling, and Ali realized, if the enemy reached the walls, the battle would take another direction. Panic started spreading among Roulan and Nora's team with all the arrows coming from the ladders. Nora kept screaming, "Use your shield to protect your lives!"

Roulan ducked below her shield and asked Ali, "Should we open the gate? Alighieri can block them!"

Ali felt that his enemy hadn't shown all of his cards, but the rebels were out of options, and Ali needed to make a call, so he ended up asking Nora to send the signal to Keita and Arsalan.

The fifteen hundred soldiers came out from the hill, running in symmetric lines and screaming. The enemy's soldiers heard it and were distracted. They didn't know whether to keep climbing or return to face the attackers.

Relief came to Nora when the arrows stopped. She then ordered her team to be prepared against those on the ladders. Keita and Arsalan finally arrived. They commanded Mamadu, and his five hundred men to take care of the climbers whose sides weren't protected. The arrows pierced them, and they started falling like flies.

Arsalan and his thousand men finally arrived and had to deal with an army bigger than his. it wasn't a fair fight, but it didn't matter for the Free People. They were focusing on one thing: fighting for their freedom.

Ali returned to his dilemma. Even if he sent Alighieri's team, they would still be outnumbered.

While he was still drowning in his thoughts, he heard a horn from the west. It was unusual to his ear, but Nadufa screamed from downstairs, "That's my brother's horn!"

It was an army of more than two thousand men coming to the rescue, they joined with no formalities so the battle continued. Keita cut his first opponent from the belly; two came at him he kicked one of them, throwing him onto his friend, and they both fell. Keita cut one's throat, and the other from between his legs.

Arsalan was enjoying his ax, moving like a snake among his enemy and all he needed was one shot to kill a Unionist.

Ali was watching from above, enjoying the victory he was about to taste, but Sai came next to him with a parchment in his hand and said, "Ali, there's something strange. I measured the surface they were standing on, it's too small to hold twenty thousand men?"

"What are you saying?"

"The maximum this surface can hold is twelve thousand!" replied Sai.

Ali looked shocked and said, "That explains why Vlad isn't with them," then he screamed, "Alighieri, Open the gate! We're going in."

Ali gave the exact same instructions to the girls.

Sai's assumption was correct. A fresh army came out of the horizon, wearing the Union's uniform and galloping toward the Free People.

John was glad to see Ali joining him and said, "We lost so many, and I don't think we can stand against this number."

Ali knew his ally wasn't wrong at all, as they were not only going to face a bigger and fresh army than theirs, but it was led by Vlad; a fierce warrior and a great tactician in war. Ali had only one suitable answer for John, "I'm truly honored to die fighting next to you."

John smiled and said, "And so are we!" Then yelled, "Take as many as you can before you die!"

They formed ranks, and the archers started shooting. With the Unionist's shields, no arrow could pass. Vlad and his army galloped towards them, pointing spears and protecting their bodies with shields.

The clash finally happened. Vlad was very excited to carry a giant sword and a triangular shield. Although his hits were slow, they were so strong; cutting every opponent coming his way. When his sword missed, his shield didn't, killing more than twenty-five soldiers without being touched. He instructed his soldiers to keep Ali busy to avoid facing him. They succeeded because every time Ali finished with an opponent, another five or six cornered him, they still couldn't touch him.

Nora wasn't carrying any shield. Rather two swords, one to block the opponent and the other to cut. Unlike Roulan, who was using her shield not just to protect herself, but also to hit her enemy with it in the neck.

Alighieri wanted to reverse the balance to their side and looked for Vlad. He knew if he took him down, his army would slack, and luckily he succeeded in cornering him.

They were face-to-face. The military chief had never seen or heard of Alighieri, who ran toward him with his sword, but Vlad wasn't as easy as Alighieri expected. He blocked his knock and deflected it with the edge of his shield, while Alighieri turned quickly and used his left elbow to hit his opponent in the back. Then he kicked him until he fell.

Vlad realized that his chances were meager with such a knight as Alighieri, so he screamed, "Soldiers, shoot this bastard," and two arrows pierced Solumy's body.

Vlad stood and commanded the two soldiers to finish his opponent, who was wounded in his shoulder and leg, kneeling with his sword in his right hand. The two soldiers couldn't approach him, so one of them took a spear to hurl it at Alighieri's heart. Luckily Keita wasn't far. He picked up his dagger and shot with all his strength at one of them, and Roulan cut the second soldier's head.

Keita came running and knelt before Alighieri, "My friend, don't worry, I'm going to get you to a safe place."

Alighieri held his friend's hand, "Don't worry, it's not very deep. Break the arrow and go help our people. I can protect myself."

Ali watched as his army vanished; he couldn't do a thing. He kept fighting and didn't care to die. In his heart, he felt there must be other rebels somewhere who would carry on his work.

Things got even worse, when he heard the land vibrating against his feet. When he looked over, there was another army with The Union's uniform coming as reinforcement to Vlad.

It didn't matter to him as long as he stuck to what he believed in, with his friends, until the end.

The army finally joined. There were at least five thousand soldiers. Both sides stopped fighting and were looking at this new army. Vlad spoke to one of his leaders, "Whose army is this?"

The leader spoke, "They are ours, but I can't see who is leading them."

The five thousand joiners began attacking Vlad's army. Ali was shocked and couldn't understand until he spotted their leader. It was a tall girl with black hair and gray eyes. Ali felt he knew her but had difficulties remembering. Unlike Vlad, who knew who she was and started screaming, "Form ranks and use shields," they all started running toward the wall and forming lines.

The joiners' leader asked her soldiers to stop fighting. She went to Ali, who was agape, "Leah sent you her wishes," she said.

Hearing her voice made Ali remember who she was. Sofia, Peter's daughter!

"I can find no words to express my gratitude, Lady Sofia," said Ali.

"You mean a lot to Leah, and she's my friend," replied Sofia and pointed her finger to Nora, "You must be the Token princess, the one who took down nine commanders on her own. Since I heard that, I was keen to meet you in person"

"You're more than welcome, Lady Sofia," replied Nora and continued, "If you want, you could join the girls' team? We're playing against the boys."

Sofia looked perplexed, and Roulan clarified, "See, these guys," she pointed toward Keita and Arsalan, then continued, "They mock us all the time, so we want to challenge them. Whoever kills the highest number of Unionists wins the challenge."

Arsalan, in shock, interrupted, "We have never mocked you. We just said the way you both fight is cute!"

"That's worse than mockery!" replied Sofia and asked, "I'd love to participate. What's the score?"

Keita boasted, "Boys are winning with seventy-two to fifty-three."

"We'll catch up soon!" replied Sofia with a wink.

Vlad was standing in front of his army about half a mile away from the Free People. He no longer had the advantage of numbers, and realized their chances were alike. He couldn't afford to lose, because even if he managed to survive Ali's sword and run, Ceres will not spare him.

Ali saw the hesitation and wanted to take advantage of it, so he suggested sparing the bloodshed and negotiating terms with Vlad. Everyone favored this proposal.

Empire of Rebels: Rise of Rebels

Sofia, Nadufa, and Alighieri accompanied Ali to the center between the two armies, and Vlad did the same with the two commanders.

When they met, Vlad spat on the ground and gave an angry look to Sofia. "You have your mother's dirty blood and your father's cowardice."

Sofia held her anger and chose not to respond, but Ali did, "If you speak again to her like that, I'll cut your throat." Then continued with a question, "What are your terms?"

"Surrender yourself, and we shall leave your army unharmed," sneered Vlad.

Ali exchanged a smile with Alighieri and replied, "You had no power to ask for that; your soldiers are exhausted and outnumbered."

Vlad replied, "Half of your men are clumsy, and can't carry a weapon properly."

Ali decided to cut to the chase, "You and I fight. If I lose, we'll surrender, if not, you walk away."

Vlad would never accept such a deal because facing Ali alone was a suicide. Instead, he turned to his soldiers and laughed loudly, "I can't make myself equal to a dirty blood who once was a slave. And even if I wanted to, the Gods forbid it!"

Sofia knew that the military chief was scared and had the right to be. Only a fool would consider fighting the legendary gladiator who never lost. Still, she liked the idea of a duel, to spare thousands of lives from the two armies, and surprised everyone when she suggested,

"Then, it's going to be you and I! My house is Yagut. Unless you're afraid to fight?"

Vlad couldn't be happier. He always hated her father and had executed her mother himself, so he accepted the proposal and went to his army to deliver the new terms and prepare.

On the other side, an argument started between Eliot and Sofia.

"You think I'm weak and not worthy to fight this dog," said Sofia.

Eliot tried to hold her hand, but she didn't let him, so he said, "I can't afford losing you!"

"Why do you assume I will lose?"

"I have never seen you fighting," said Eliot.

"What?"

"Sorry, I mean, you're an excellent fighter, but I won't take the slightest risk of losing you!" replied Eliot.

Sofia was touched by his words, so she lowered her tone and said, "I know how important I am to you, because I feel the same way toward you. But this is a golden opportunity to spare all these lives!"

Eliot tried his best but couldn't change her decision. Although he knew she might lose her life, he held her by the shoulder and said, "Fine, I respect your decision. Bring us the victory of life."

Ali didn't like the idea, but Sofia persuaded him and explained that she was as good as Princess Leah.

Nora and Roulan insisted on taking Sofia to the walls and changing her uniform, making her wear one that represented the Free People. It consisted of black boots, gray leather trousers, and a red top made from mithril. They tied her hair with a band, and Sofia added a protective helmet.

The armies approached the battlefield, where Sofia and Vlad stood face to face. Nadufa gave the signal to start.

They were both staring at each other and moving left and right, trying to find a good spot to attack.

Vlad chose words to distract her, "I'll grant you a favor by killing you. After all, you have your mother's dirty blood, who couldn't even produce a boy for Peter to pass on his legacy."

It didn't work on her, and she kept staring at him. Then he raised his tone, "I was thrilled when his highness assigned me your mother's execution. I tortured her for a while, until she begged me to kill her, and I did."

This time, Vlad's words reached her. Ali screamed, "He's trying to distract you! Focus on the fight."

Sofia ignored the advice and ran towards Vlad, attacking with her sword. But her opponent was defending himself properly. He placed his left hand behind his back and fought with one hand, pretending to be on the defense. After several knocks, he switched to an attacking mode with heavier hits.

On the ninth knock, he fetched a dagger with his other hand and slashed at Sofia's neck. She tried to avoid it, but it was quick and touched her neck. Fortunately, it wasn't deep. Eliot advanced, but Ali held his arm to stop him.

Sofia passed her hand over the injury and became angrier when she saw the blood.

She sprinted again next to her opponent, who this time was in an attack mode with his sword. While their hands were blocking each other, he pushed her and kicked her in the belly. Sofia getting distracted. He went with his sword to cut her head off, but he missed the neck and hit her head.

Luckily, she was wearing a helmet. But still, she fell on the ground feeling strong vertigo. She looked at Ali and saw his frightened face, then stood and took a fighting position.

Sofia decided to throw away her sword and fetched her favorite weapons, two daggers, and ran again towards Vlad. He was expecting her with his sword, but before the clash, she threw a dagger at him. By the time he blocked it with his sword, Sofia had already arrived, Vlad stopped her blade using his sword and, Peter's daughter fetched a third one from her boot and touched his arm, then rolled over to the other side.

A scream came from Ali's army.

"Nora!" shouted Sofia.

The Token girl immediately threw a bayonet. It was like a spear, but its two ends had sharp blades.

Sofia fetched it and started rolling it around her wrist, trying to intimidate Vlad who attacked this time. Sofia took a defensive position, blocking his sword, and whenever he tried with his dagger, she pivoted her weapon to stop it.

Ali understood her tactic. She was taking advantage of his deep injury, trying to exhaust him, and it was working. She surprised him by lowering her bayonet to his right foot and hit his leg, then rolled over and hit his other leg.

With a groan, Vlad's knees buckled beneath him, yet still, he clutched tightly to his sword. Sofia paid him no mind and pressed forward for the killing blow. On the third strike, Vlad's sword slipped from his grasp and clattered to the ground, as his opponent triumphantly removed her helmet, revealing a cascade of brown curls that tumbled down her shoulders. Ali, standing beside Eliot, was rooted to the spot, utterly speechless.

"I told you I will kill you myself". Said Vlad's killer.

Vlad was paralyzed from shock. All he could say was, "Princess Leah!"

Indeed ,she was the princess, who had fooled everyone into thinking that Sofia would face Vlad while it was her. She did it because she knew the military chief would never accept a fight with Ceres' daughter. She went behind him and passed the blade of her dagger over his neck slowly, the monster Vlad was slain.

Ali's heart could've pumped out of his chest from the joy of seeing Leah, coming towards him. A smile went wider on his face, and he said, "You came to my rescue even though I asked you not to."

"You're not a king to command me!" said Leah and added, "Yet."

Keita asked, "How could you fool all of us? And why?"

Leah smiled, "Well, Nora and Roulan helped us to trick everyone! I didn't want my father to know that I joined you."

Arsalan interrupted, "But you revealed yourself, and now they all know you fought against the empire!"

"When I was about to start fighting Vlad, I turned and saw you all looking at me with eyes full of life and hope to see a better world. I realized that this is where I belong, with Ali and you. As for my father, he's wrong!" replied Leah.

The screaming of the Free People filled the area, but Ali raised his hand and asked to get prepared. He was afraid that the Union's commanders would not hold their promise. Luckily, he was wrong. Two of them advanced next to the body of Vlad, and Ali joined them with Arsalan and Nadufa.

One of the commanders said, "We're men of our word. We'll leave, but the next time we come, we'll tear down these walls."

Ali understood that the commander was talking out of rage and chose to smile. Then he promised to bury their dead properly.

Before Ali and his friends got in the castle to celebrate their victory, Keita addressed Nora and Roulan,

"Ladies, I think you have some acknowledgments to do,"

Everyone stared at him and Arsalan clarified, "He meant the challenge between girls and boys."

"That's right, seventy-two to fifty-three. We won" added Keita.

Nora and Roulan grimaced and said nothing. But Alighieri did.

"Vlad counts for a hundred. The girls won."

Chapter 28

It took five days for the Free People to get rid of the dead bodies. They held their promise to the commanders and buried the Union's dead. They had to carry them in wagons about three miles away.

As for their own, there were more than a thousand corpses, men and women. They were buried in a cemetery in front of the wall. On each grave, they engraved their names, their house, and the nickname their beloved ones chose for him or her.

Ali gathered his six friends, Nadufa, John, Leah, and her friend, to discuss what was coming. After some routine discussions, he started, "I don't know if you realize what we have achieved, but we took down an army of twenty thousand Union soldiers. This is so huge that history won't forget it for thousands of years, but remember…"

"If it weren't for Leah and Sofia, we'd all be dead," interrupted Alighieri.

"What matters now is the result! Which is an epic victory!" replied Ali.

Leah added, "You should give yourself some credit. If you and your six friends weren't great, I would never have come to your rescue."

Alighieri nodded with a smile and Ali continued, "We poked a giant bear with the power of more than a hundred thousand soldiers, and honestly, I knew Ceres and Ramessess very well. They're not to be underestimated. The next time they attack, they'll be much more prepared to destroy us."

John stood and added, "Ali is right. The emperor is a very determined man, surrounded by clever advisors. He will design a plan to invade us if we're not very cautious. "

"Thank you, John," Ali replied, "First, we need to nominate a king for the Free People."

All the attendees looked at each other and started smiling, and Nora intervened, "Isn't that obvious? I mean, it's you."

All the others agreed, and Ali interrupted them, "As much as I appreciate your trust, I'd like to remind you, that I'm not a legitimate king. My ancestors had never ruled. People usually revolt against a leader with no royal blood."

Nadufa was a wise woman and knew what kind of man Ali was. His heart was empty of greed for power or wealth. On the contrary, she thought he was a man who considered power as a heavy burden, so she wanted to ease the task, "Maybe we're not yet in a position to nominate a king or queen yet. What if instead, we agree on one man to lead us to victory, and after that, we can think of who will rule us officially." Without waiting for his response, she asked, "Who is in favor that Lord Ali leads us for the time being?"

Everyone raised their hand except for Leah and Sofia. So John asked, "Who would you choose, ladies?"

"We don't consider ourselves as one of you. Remember, I'm your enemy's daughter," replied Leah.

A peal of laughter filled the room, and Nora said, "You're stuck with us!"

And as easily as that, Ali became the Free People's leader.

"What's your command, Lord Ali?" asked Alighieri.

They were all looking at him with smiles on their faces.

"We can't stay here any longer. The cold and darkness won't help us, so I'm suggesting preparing our armies," he stopped, and his friends were silent, waiting for him to continue. He grinned. "We need a new land!"

Printed in Great Britain
by Amazon